"What's happening tomorrow?"

His fingers skimmed her palm. "Our first kiss."

"Really."

"Yeah. First thing." He winked at her. "So tell me when it's midnight."

"I'm nobody's timekeeper, Trace."

"Look at me." He waited for Skyler's full attention, which she granted. "Right here, right now, you and me. One kiss to start the day. It's my birthday." He glanced at her watch. "It's midnight."

"Happy birthday." She tipped her head and leaned close to bestow a friendly kiss.

He slid his arm around her and met her halfway, raising the ante on her gift by making it interactive, taking her breath away. She trembled inside when he lifted his head and looked at her with a twinkle in his eyes that said "Gotcha."

Dear Reader,

"Cowboy, Take Me Away" is an incredibly romantic song recorded by the Dixie Chicks. The title itself conjures an image silhouetted against a painted Western sky—two lovers on one magnificent horse taking the long way home.

Trace and Skyler are about as different as two people can be, but they have at least one thing in common: each lives in a house that doesn't feel like home. They meet in the heat of summer, when excitement runs higher, hearts beat faster and risks are easier to take because it's rodeo season. Can a cautious woman like Skyler allow herself to be taken away from a world that holds no promise for her by a man who makes his living "going down the road"?

Well, maybe for a day or two.

Happy reading!

Kathleen Eagle

COWBOY, TAKE ME AWAY

KATHLEEN EAGLE

Harlequin®

SPECIAL EDITION

Recycling programs
for this product may
not exist in your area.

ISBN-13: 978-0-373-65595-3

COWBOY, TAKE ME AWAY

Copyright © 2011 by Kathleen Eagle

www.Harlequin.com

Printed in U.S.A.

KATHLEEN EAGLE

published her first book, a Romance Writers of America Golden Heart Award winner, with Silhouette Books in 1984. Since then she has published more than forty books, including historical and contemporary, series and single title, earning her nearly every award in the industry. Her books have consistently appeared on regional and national bestseller lists, including the *USA TODAY* list and the *New York Times* extended bestseller list.

Kathleen lives in Minnesota with her husband, who is Lakota Sioux. They have three grown children and three lively grandchildren.

For my wonderful editors,
Leslie Wainger and Charles Griemsman.

Chapter One

Skyler Quinn's viewfinder served as both protection and pretext for her hungry eye. Naked, her eye was never more than mildly interested. Behind the camera, it was appreciative of all things bright and beautiful. The viewfinder found and framed views she had schooled herself to ignore, like the rear view of five fine-looking cowboys hooked over a fence. She would call the shot *Five Perfect Pairs of Jeans.*

And then there were four.

Skyler lowered the camera. The best pair of jeans was getting away. Up one side of the fence and down the other, the cowboy on the far left had spoiled the symmetry of her shot. She climbed a set of wooden steps and took a position on the first landing of the outdoor grandstand, where an audience would later gather to watch professional rodeo cowboys ride, rope and race for cash prizes. For now, the place belonged to cowboys, critters and one unobtrusive camera.

Skyler watched the runaway piece of her picture stride purposefully across the dusty arena toward one of several ropers who were warming up to compete in the afternoon "slack" for overflow timed-event contestants. The roper responded to a quick gesture as though he'd been summoned by the coach.

Skyler zoomed in as the two men changed places. She knew horses, and the blazed-face sorrel hadn't been working for his rider, but the animal collected himself immediately with a new man in the saddle. The camera committed the subtleties of change to its memory card. Eyes, ears, carriage, gait—the animal transformed from ordinary to outstanding before Skyler's hidden eye.

Now, that's what I'm talking about.

Or *would* talk about when she got around to putting a story together. The centaur lived, she would claim. He was no freak of nature, anything but barbaric, and beyond comparison with a mere horse master. He was a partner. He shared his brainpower with the horse and the horse gave him legs. It was a pleasing blend of assets, particularly when both partners were beautifully supplied. Not only would her pictures tell the story, but they could sell the story. Most horse magazines were bought and read by women, and here was a man who would stop any girl's thumb-through dead in its tracks. Long, lean, lithe and leggy, he was made to ride. The square chin and chiseled jaw were promising, but she wished he would push his hat back a little so she could see more of his face.

Skyler kept her distance as she followed the cowboy through his ride. She supposed he was giving a demonstration—teaching, selling, maybe considering a purchase. A cowboy with a good roping horse often "mounted" other ropers for a share of their winnings, but the sorrel didn't fit the bill. She wondered what the cowboy said to the original rider after his smooth dismount. Deal, no deal, or a word of advice? She'd be interested in the man's advice. Lately she'd been learning the difference between horse master—that would be Skyler—and master trainer, which she was not. *Yet.*

At the moment she was interested in taking pictures. She clambered down the grandstand steps and strolled toward the exit, eyeing a long shot down an alley where two palominos were visiting across a portable panel fence. The rodeo wasn't Skyler's favorite venue, but horses and horsemen were among her favorite subjects for her second-favorite hobby. And it was high time she turned at least one of her hobbies into an income-earning proposition.

"Business or pleasure?"

Skyler turned to the sound of a deep, smooth voice and looked directly into engaging gold-brown eyes. Unexpected, unshielded, up close and personal. *There you are,* said her heart. "I beg your pardon?" said her mouth.

"You were taking pictures of me." His eyes hinted at some amusement, but no uncertainty. "Are you a professional or a fan?"

Skyler's brain cartwheeled over her other body parts and took charge.

"I don't know you, but I know horse sense when I see it, and I like to take pictures." She smiled. His face complemented his body—long, slender, neatly groomed, ready for a close-up. "I wouldn't mind getting paid to do it, but at the moment, it's merely my pleasure."

"Taking pictures of…horse sense."

She turned the camera on, pressed a button and turned the display his way. "Would you like to see?"

He clicked through her pictures. "You've got a powerful zoom there. Look at that." He stepped closer and shared a peek. "You can see where I nicked myself shaving this morning."

"I don't see anything."

"Luckily, it's just my face. No harm done to the horse sense."

"It's a valuable asset." She nodded toward the picture on the camera display. *Commanding Cowboy on a Collected Mount.* "Do you have an interest in this horse?"

"I might buy him." He studied the picture, considering. "If the price is right. This guy's trying to take him in the wrong direction. He's not a roping horse. He's small and he's quick." Their fingers touched as he handed the camera back. She bit back an apology and a cliché about cold hands. His warmth reached his eyes. "Make a nice cuttin' horse."

"You're a trainer?" *Obviously.*

"I'm a bronc rider. Got no sense at all." He tucked his thumbs into the front pockets of his jeans. "You coming to the show tonight?"

"I haven't decided." She was committed to watching the ropers in the afternoon slack, which moments ago had seemed like enough rodeo for one day.

"You'd get some good pictures."

"I'm not your *Rodeo Sports News* kind of photographer. And I'm really not interested in the kind of ride that only lasts eight seconds."

"Only?" He laughed. "That's eight *real* seconds. You know you're alive when every second really means something. How many seconds like that can you stand, one right after another?"

"I feel very much alive on the back of a horse. I could go all day."

He took her point with a nod, eyes dancing. "They say when you meet your match, time stands still. You believe that?"

"I think your idea of the perfect match is different from mine."

"What do you look for?"

"A great ride."

"Same here. You say *girth* and I say *cinch,* but,

hell, we're both horse people. If you're thirsty, I know a good watering hole that's probably pretty quiet this time of day. First round's on me."

"That's very tempting, but I have to…" Not really. There was nothing she had to do in Sheridan, Wyoming. If she'd come on her own, she could watch the afternoon calf roping and go home, where she always had things to do. "Are you competing in the rodeo tonight?" He nodded. "Which event?"

"Bareback." He pushed his right hand deep into his jeans pocket. "I've got an extra ticket. One is all I've got, so if you're with somebody…"

"No, I'm…" But she took the ticket he handed her and inspected it as though she hadn't seen one before. "I mean, I haven't decided. I wouldn't want this to go to waste."

She looked up to find him grinning as he backed away. "You should see my horse sense in a pair of chaps. Bring your camera."

She met his grin with a smile. "You cowboys are all alike."

"I won't ask how many you know. You can tell me tonight when you come by the chutes to wish me luck."

"I don't even know your name."

"It'll be on the program." Safely out of returning-the-ticket distance, he paused. "You gonna tell me yours?"

"I haven't decided. And I'm not on the program."

* * *

Trace wasn't holding his breath. The woman was as intriguing as she was beautiful, and her showing up behind the chutes or even in the stands was a long shot, which was what made the bet interesting. Surprise was the spice of Trace Wolf Track's life.

He hadn't always seen it that way, but he'd lived and he'd learned. Life was full of surprises, people were totally unpredictable and a guy could either try to buck the system or enjoy the ride. Sure, he searched the crowd for that pretty face once or twice, and he turned his head to the sound of a female voice just before he lowered himself into the chute and took hold of his bareback rigging.

And then he cursed himself for losing his concentration when he should have been calling for the gate. He'd drawn a chute fighter. *No screwing around, cowboy. I'm outta here, with or without you.*

Trace made the whistle, but his signature dismount turned ugly in the face of a flying hoof. He didn't mind getting clipped in the head, but mentally he took points off his score for stumbling and losing his hat. Winning a go-round wasn't everything. He scanned the bleachers as he acknowledged the applause with a wave of the errant hat. He had no idea where to look for the seat he'd given her, but did a double take at the sight of a pretty woman in the front row jumping to her feet.

He had to laugh at himself when the woman reached across the aisle and took a toddler from somebody's arms. Not his ticket holder. The hair was too yellow, the hips were too broad and the kid appeared to be hers. He'd been thinking about his green-eyed photographer with the reddish-blond hair all afternoon, recalling her sweet scent, guessing her name and making up her story. It didn't include kids.

Trace unbuckled his chaps as he ambled back to the chutes. He wiped his head with his shirtsleeve. Sure enough, the hoof had drawn blood, which he didn't mind getting on his shirt, but he hated like hell messing up the sponsor's patch on the sleeve. He'd sold his right arm to promote cigarettes. Took the money and quit smoking, thanks to the bloody patch.

He put his hat back on for a dignified departure. Exiting the arena on the heels of a good score required cowboy reserve. Win or lose, the slight swagger in his step came from years of forking a horse nearly every day. Ordinarily he would have been mentally downshifting now that his workday was over—one man's eight seconds was another's eight hours—and it was time to celebrate, whether he felt like it or not.

"Nice ride," said saddle bronc rider Larry Mossbrucker as he caught up with Trace on the way to the medic's van. "Where's the party tonight?"

"Haven't heard."

"It's your call, man. First round's on the winner." Larry clapped a beefy hand on Trace's shoulder.

"Bob's? You don't wanna miss BOGO Burger Night."

The only thing worse than one of Bob's Bronc Buster burgers would be a second Bronc Buster burger, but the place would be packed to the gills on Bob's stuffed-and-mounted trophy trout.

"Think I'll pass on the gut busters. Busted enough for one day. But I'll stop in and pony up after I clean up and get something to eat." Trace glanced at Larry, who looked disappointed. "Something that won't bite back."

"How's the head?"

"I'm keepin' it under my hat."

"Aw, man, don't let a fresh wound go to waste. That's good for unlimited female sympathy. A rare treat. Tender." Larry grinned. "Juicy."

"Mmm. I can taste it already. But that kind of meal don't come cheap and they don't give a free one on top of it." Trace eased his hat off. The sweatband was killing him. "'Course you don't need it when the first one's that good."

"Yeah, well, you gotta do a few shots between burgers at Bob's."

"Should be good for unlimited sympathy all around."

"They started burger night after they had to quit Ladies' Night." Larry was keeping pace with Trace, who wasn't in the mood for much conversation, which meant he wasn't in the mood for Larry.

But Larry was a talker.

"Some tourist said it wasn't right to charge men more than women. Discrimination, he called it. Maybe they've got a big supply of women where he comes from, but out here the good ones are scarce, and no shortage of demand. No shortage of bars or beer, either, so which law should we go by? Supply and demand, or whatever it is that outlaws discrimination?"

Trace chuckled. "My guess, it's that ol' killjoy, the U.S. Constitution."

"The only woman willing to go to Bob's for a free burger would have to be another tourist."

"With an iron gut. Hell, Bob's not hurtin' for business and we ain't hurtin' for women."

Larry snorted. "Speak for yourself."

He *was*.

Another twenty yards and Trace would be speaking to the rodeo medic about whether he needed stitches, and he wouldn't be expressing any more interest than he was feeling when he asked, "Angie kicked you out again?"

"Hell, no. She's letting me sleep on the sofa." Larry gave an unconvincing chuckle. "Hell, when I first met her, she was all about being with a cowboy. Now she wants me to quit riding."

"Gotta quit sometime." While you're ahead. *While your head is ahead.*

"Not me, boy. Not till I'm damn good and ready." They'd reached the "Cowboy Clinic" van and Larry was dragging his heels like a pouty kid. "Hell, I don't know what else I'd do."

"This is where I get off, Larry. Maybe I'll catch up with you at Bob's."

Larry nodded, but he wasn't moving.

"Where are you staying?" The question was out before Trace could stop himself. He knew the answer. Larry hadn't scored in the money, and he was nobody's favorite road warrior, so he had to be sleeping single in his pickup.

"Put it this way, there's no running water," Larry said.

"Come on over to the Sheridan Inn. I got myself a room this time out."

"I wouldn't wanna put you out, Trace. That's a fancy place."

"I know. All I'm offering is soap and water." Trace tapped the big man's chest with the back of his hand. "You don't wanna out-reek Bob's burgers."

Trace topped off his steak by washing down a few aspirin and left the hotel dining room hoping Larry hadn't left the bathroom in a mess. Trace didn't mind sharing—he'd been raised to share—but he'd also been taught to clean up after himself, especially when he was sharing a room or a bed. Growing up he'd shared a low-end range of small quarters and smaller beds with his younger brother, Ethan, who'd never done well with rules. Cleaning up after Ethan had taught Trace a corollary to the clean-up rule.

People should do it for themselves. Otherwise, each mess was a little harder to deal with than the last. Leaving a mess in the bathroom had become a deal breaker for sharing a room with Trace. But he'd still make an exception for his brother. All Ethan had to do was show up.

Or the camera lady. She could drop her towel on Trace's bathroom floor anytime. He hadn't expected her to use the ticket, but he knew damn well she'd given it some thought. No matter what her circumstances, he knew he'd caught more than her eye. And she'd sure stimulated his imagination. If a woman like her went out on the town, where would he find her? Provided he felt like looking for a woman who smelled like an orange tree standing in the middle of a horse barn. Pretty risky for a horse-barn kind of a guy.

He was on his way to the hotel bar and a shot of pain reliever when he ran into calf roper Mike Quinn, who said he was buying. He could have sworn Mike wasn't old enough to get served, but his driver's license said he was legal. Barely. Trace had just finished turning up Mike's roping horse, a sideline that was becoming increasingly profitable.

"I owe you one," Mike said as he smacked his cash down on the bar as though he had a point to make. "Eleven-two, man, that's the fastest run I've made all summer. You put a hell of a handle on that horse."

"That's what you paid me for."

Trace stepped aside for a lady looking for a barstool. He wouldn't be riding one of those tonight. With a rodeo in town, one drink in a fancy hotel bar was all he was good for. If he could get past his headache, he'd find the party down at the low end of Main Street on the other side of the tracks.

"I know what you're thinking," Mike said quietly. He'd suddenly gone shy. "The horse did his part, but the roper's a little slow on the ground."

Trace lifted one shoulder. "You drew a big calf."

"Caught him, too, but *damn* them doggies're getting heavy. Now that you've got my horse lined out, I'm gonna have to get myself a personal trainer. I don't suppose you'd…"

"I only work with horses. Cowboys can be temperamental." But they didn't call calves *doggies* anymore. Mike needed to put some new tunes on his iPod.

"Not this cowboy. Win or lose, I celebrate." Mike was pushing it, laying his novice hand on Trace's proven shoulder. The kid had a lot to learn before he could rightly call himself a cowboy. "Whatever you're drinking tonight, it's on me. Frank Taggert's here and Earl Kessler. You know Earl?"

"I don't."

"Earl has a big spread over on the Powder River. I belong to a team-penning club that meets at his place. You should check us out. We've got guys coming from as far away as Casper."

"I haven't played team sports since high school." And he damn sure wasn't interested in driving a hundred miles or more to play cowboy. Not that he had anything against the popularity of team penning. He'd trained a couple of cutting horses for penning club members.

"Earl's place is kinda central, easy to get to, he doesn't charge us to use his stock, and he always fires up the grill and ices down the beer. I fixed him up for dinner tonight." Mike laughed. "With my mother. You believe that?"

Trace glanced up from his drink, ready for some weird punch line. Mike had a weird sense of humor.

The kid shrugged. "My dad's been dead a year now and it's time she moved on. So to speak."

Trace remembered a time when he'd hoped for a new dad. Not that he'd missed the old one, whoever he was, but at the age of ten he'd imagined his mother doing a better job of mothering if she hooked up with a man who'd stick around. He couldn't have asked for better than Logan Wolf Track, who'd stuck by Trace and his brother even after their mother had walked out on all of them. So Mike had just earned a few points in Trace's book for looking after his lonely mother.

Glancing past Trace's shoulder, Mike frowned. "Speak of the devil…"

Trace suddenly felt a little buzzed and he knew the whiskey wasn't *that* potent. He turned slowly. She was a willowy silhouette standing in the doorway, backlit by the bright lobby. He suddenly got all tingly.

Strangest, most godawful giddy sensation he could imagine, partly because he knew who she was, knew she was surprised to see him even though he couldn't quite make out her face.

"That's your *mother?*"

"Stepmother," Mike said quietly as they watched her approach them at the bar, at once purposeful and unhurried. "But I don't like that term. Sounds cold, y'know?"

"Cold as the devil." Trace nodded, inadvertently lifting his hand to touch a hat brim that wasn't there. "Mrs. Quinn."

"Trace Wolf Track," she said, eyes alight. "Your name was on the program."

"You were there?"

"How else was I going to get a program?" She smiled. "You were magnificent."

"Thanks." *Magnificent.* Damn.

"For eight whole seconds."

"Just a sample. Imagine eight whole hours."

Her quick laugh was throaty and rich. "You're all alike."

Trace raised one eyebrow and challenged her with a look. *Try me.*

"Looks like we can skip the introductions," Mike said.

"Only if your mother likes to be called Mrs. Quinn." But Mike could skip town now for all Trace cared. He only had eyes and ears for...

"Skyler."

"This is the guy who trained Bit-o-Honey," Mike supplied. "You wrote the check. Remember?"

Trace glanced down at the glass in his hand. He'd hardly looked at the check. Counted the zeros, copied them onto the deposit slip. Why did it feel funny knowing that she'd been the one who'd paid him?

"I'm the bookkeeper." She gave a honeyed laugh. "Names might escape me, but I never forget an expense category."

"You remembered mine from the program."

"I had a face to put with it." She turned to her son. *Step*son. "I was taking pictures at the arena this afternoon, and Trace and I...crossed paths."

Trace slid her a smile.

"What happened to Earl?" Mike demanded, glancing toward the lobby.

Skyler stabbed Mike's arm with a small but forceful forefinger. "The question is, what happened to you?"

"I told you guys to go ahead and get supper. I'm toasting my trainer here."

"Were you invited to Mike's party, too?" she asked Trace.

"I was offered a drink." He lifted his half-full glass. "I'm a long way from getting toasted."

She claimed Trace's drink and mirrored his gesture. "Here's to Mike and his trainer."

Down the hatch.

She set the empty glass aside and took number two from Mike's hand, flashing an enticing glance at Trace as she raised the glass. "And to Trace Wolf Track and his impressive horse sense."

Down the hatch.

Glass on wood, she called out, "Bartender! Another round for these two cowboys."

"Okay, she's mad now," Mike told Trace.

"Not anymore." Skyler gave Mike a perfunctory smile. "If you aren't having dinner with Earl, you might want to tell him he's excused."

"I was coming back."

"You were on your way back, but you ran into a couple of buddies, and one drink led to another." She shifted from script reader to instructor. "Earl doesn't interest me. Nothing about Earl interests me. I had a wonderful time at the rodeo, Mike. You interest me because you're my son. Trace interests me because he's…interesting." She spared Trace a pointed glance. "Earl does not interest me."

"But he's got—"

"I don't care what he's got. You don't have to worry about me. Okay?" She shrugged dismissively. "And if this is a celebration, I'm not feeling it."

"One more oughta do it." Mike gave a nod for the two drinks the bartender was just setting down near his elbow.

"You know what?" Trace pulled a couple of bills from his pocket and tossed them on the bar. "In the interest of mutual interest—" he turned to Skyler and smiled "—why don't we hold off and take a walk?"

"What about Earl?" Mike demanded.

Trace laid a friendly hand on Mike's beefy shoulder. "I'd say Earl is your problem, son."

"Son?"

"You make a date, it's yours to keep, yours to break."

"Impressive," Skyler said. "Who trained the trainer?"

"My dad. Logan Wolf Track is the best there is." He gestured toward the exit with a flourish. *After you.* "What's your pleasure tonight, Mrs. Quinn?"

"Do you dance?"

"Hell, yeah, like nobody's watching. You know any cowboys who don't?" He offered his arm. "Mrs. Quinn?"

"Mrs. Quinn doesn't remember how to dance like nobody's watching." She slipped her hand into the crook of his elbow and smile up at him. "But let's see if Skyler does."

Chapter Two

There was a sweet sensuality about the way Trace held her when they danced—not hard, not tight, but close enough to feel the power in his thighs and the heat in his belly and the cool in his carriage. Her body moved with his, riding double on a silky new song. New for Skyler, anyway. She hadn't danced in ages, which was not a measure of time, but a chunk of life. She felt lighter on her feet than she had in ages, lighter in heart and head. Giddy-light, something a man like Trace would know nothing about. She felt so new she was afraid if she opened her mouth she'd squeal with delight or babble some kind of gibberish and he'd have no interest in a translation. So she kept quiet and rode her senses, her thighs glancing off his, her nose sneaking up on his neck, her ears tuning in to the drums and the steel guitar.

Given the kind of erotic thoughts she'd been having lately, it was probably pretty risky for her to let a man who smelled this good get this close, but she was sure she had the upper hand. She was a woman, after all. She knew how to smell the flowers. Or, in this case, the alfalfa. She knew how to lose herself on a little detour, soak up some unexpected warmth and inhale the greener grass.

Close your eyes and take a long, slow breath. Let the picture draw itself in your mind. Pure, natural manhood.

Now that she knew why Mike had insisted on her coming to Sheridan to watch him put his newly trained calf roping horse to the test, she had to admit, he wasn't totally off base. It felt good to "meet somebody." Not Mike's choice of somebody. Not an internet site's choice or the choice of a friend worried about her widowhood, but her own out-of-the-blue discovery. Somebody who tapped into her own senses and jangled nerves she'd tried and failed to forget she had. Not that she didn't like the feeling, but she wasn't sure she could rein it in if she gave it any slack.

"It was nice of Mrs. Quinn to let me take Skyler dancing." He leaned back and smiled at her. "Tell her for me next time you see her."

"Tell her yourself." She looked up, but not, she realized, as far up as she'd expected to. The way he carried himself made him seem taller than he was.

"Truthfully, I don't see her. Everyone else does, but I don't."

"You're like that comedian on TV, huh? He doesn't see skin color, including his own?" He chuckled. "How do you know what everyone else sees?"

"Maybe not you. Who do you see?"

"Right now, I see a woman who's enjoying herself."

"Good eye, cowboy." Wolf eyes. Tawny and teasing, they twinkled with every charming line he spoke. "Would you have fixed me up with Earl Kessler?"

"Absolutely not. And I don't know Earl Kessler." He shook his head. "I don't know what Mike was thinking. He should have fixed you up with me."

"He shouldn't be trying to fix me up at all."

"If he hadn't, would we be dancing right now?" He raised his wounded brow. "Would Mrs. Quinn have let Skyler come out to play?"

"Mrs. Quinn might have gone out with you herself. You wouldn't have been able to dance this close, but otherwise you wouldn't know the difference."

"Ah, so you *do* know her."

"I don't see her, but she was fifteen years in the making, so I know her."

He smiled again. "I only dance as close as my partner wants me to. Sometimes it's like this. Sometimes it's even closer. But I always know the difference."

"Instinctively?"

"My instincts are pretty good. I've got good ears, too."

"And you've got a good lump on your head." The knot on the right side of his temple was decorated with Steri-Strips. Without thinking, she touched the outer edge of the goose egg. "Does it hurt?"

"Only when I touch it." He laughed when she jerked her hand away. "Do that again. Your fingers feel cool."

She put her hand back in its proper place on his shoulder. "I've fallen off a horse a few times, but I've never been kicked."

"I didn't fall."

"You were unloaded."

"I made the whistle. That's what counts."

She welcomed the excuse to touch his head again. "This counts."

"That's what I've heard," he said, grinning. "I know it draws sharks, but I didn't realize blood was a chick magnet."

She laughed. "Hardly."

"Hardly attracted?"

"Hardly a chick."

"You're right. My bad." He flashed that infectious grin again. "You like 'filly bait' any better?"

"Give it up, cowboy. I like you, okay? No bloodshed necessary. Extra points for not calling me a mother hen."

Trace guided her to the corner booth they'd claimed at the Mane and Tail Tavern, one of Sheridan's quieter nightspots. Rodeo cowboys preferred Bob's Place and rodeo fans followed rodeo cowboys.

His hand on the small of her back was their only contact point, but she felt him covering her back, head to heels.

"I like you, too," he said as she took herself from him, only to slide around the vinyl curve of the seat and meet him at the back of the booth. "So let's get this out on the table. I'm not a kid. I'm not sure I ever was. I was raised by my stepfather, and he was younger than my mother. Still is if she's alive."

"You don't know?"

"I like to think she isn't." He toyed with his watered-down whiskey, spreading its sweat ring in an ever-widening circle. "I made up a story about how she was trying to get back to us when she got hit by a train. That's the only reason we never heard from her again." He sipped his drink before eyeing her. "How's that for bloodthirsty? Do I lose points?"

"She just disappeared?"

"She told us she was gonna look for a better place for us. I knew she wasn't coming back. Logan had adopted us first thing after he married her. He told her he wasn't goin' anywhere, and for a while he thought she'd come back." He smiled wistfully. "He was so damn young." His eyes suddenly gleamed. "But he was a good father, and he will be again. He just remarried. Took him a while, but, hell, when that man makes up his mind, he doesn't waste any time. I hope this one works out better for him."

"Is this one older, too?"

"Older than Logan?" He shook his head. "She's

probably not much older than me. Funny. I don't remember ever running into her, but turns out she didn't live too far away. Two different worlds, I guess. Small, side by side and different."

"Where are they?"

"South Dakota. Logan—my dad—he's Sioux. Lakota Sioux."

"You're not?"

"In name only. He offered his name when he adopted us, and we jumped on it. Who wouldn't? Wolf Track." He punctuated a tight-lipped growl with a fisted gesture. "Powerful name."

"So he's your true father."

"Oh, yeah. Taught me everything I know about horses. Not everything he knows, but everything I know."

"Is he a rodeo cowboy, too?"

"No. He's smarter than that. Logan's a tribal councilman, and he's also a horse trainer. He wrote a book about it and everything."

"You did a wonderful job with Bit-o-Honey. I can't believe he's the same horse." Skyler lifted her shoulder. "Of course, Mike's still the same rider."

"It's a good hobby for a rancher."

"He told you he was a rancher?"

Trace nodded.

"Good to know," she said offhandedly. "He tells *me* he's a calf roper."

"He's young. He can still be a lot of things."

"He'd better decide which is the hobby pretty soon, or the choice won't be there for him."

"What time is it?" Trace slid his hand over the back of hers and turned her wrist for a peek at her watch. "Almost tomorrow. Big day tomorrow."

"Bigger than today? You won your go-round today. What's happening tomorrow?"

His fingers skimmed her palm. "Our first kiss."

"Really?"

"Yeah. First thing." He winked at her. "So tell me when it's midnight."

"I'm nobody's timekeeper, Trace. Trying not to be." She gave her head a quick shake as she echoed her admonishment to him. "Give it up, Skyler."

"We're talking past each other here. Look at me." He waited for her full attention, which she granted. "Right here, right now, you and me. One kiss to start the day. It's my birthday."

"Oh." She smiled. "Well, that's different."

"*I'm* different. Give me a day to prove it."

"Why?"

"Because…" He glanced at her watch. "It's midnight."

"Happy birthday." She tipped her head and leaned close to bestow a friendly kiss.

He slid his arm around her and met her halfway, raising the ante on her gift by making it interactive, taking her breath away. Her kiss became theirs as she slid her arm around him and smoothed the back of his shirt with her eager hand. She felt trembly inside when he lifted his head and looked at her with a twinkle in his eyes that said *gotcha*.

"Spend the day with me," he entreated, and she had to glance away from those glittering eyes to keep from jumping all over the suggestion.

"What's holding you back?" He raised an eyebrow. "Tell me, and I'll get it out of your way."

"I have things to do at home."

"I'll help you. Give me one day and I'll give one back." She hesitated, and he laughed. He knew he had her, but he offered, "*Two*. I'll trade you two days for one, and I'm a damn good hand."

"Now, that's tempting." A crazy idea was taking shape in her head. Lately they'd been popping up like soap bubbles. Crazy notions pushing for bubble-headed moves. She'd made one or two, just to get herself off dead center, and she was about to make another one.

She smiled. "What can I get out of you on those days?"

"What do you need?"

"Mostly horse sense."

"Well, then, I'm mostly your man."

"I own horses, condition them, ride them, school them. I'm a natural, really. And I've had some spirited horses." She leaned into her story, trusting him with the girlish enthusiasm that was generally reserved for her horses. "So I thought, why shouldn't I be able to turn a mustang into a mild-mannered saddle horse?

We could learn from each other. Wouldn't that be interesting?"

"For me?"

"For me. I entered a training competition. But I might have bitten off more than I can chew." She lowered her gaze to his smirking lips. She could still taste them. "How are your teeth?"

"I'm not missing any, but you'll have to take the deal before I let you count 'em."

She laughed. She liked this man. She truly did. "After two days, can I have an option to hire?"

"Nope." He leaned back, challenging her with a playful look as he reached toward his glass. "Free agency after three days. Then we renegotiate."

"Sounds fair."

"It's more than sound." He gestured, glass in hand. "You're getting a twofer."

"Can't pass that up, can I?" She slapped the table. "Okay, I need to rest up for the big day."

"Oh, no. Today is my day." He drained his drink and then set the glass aside. "I get to call the shots. You play Hearts?"

"The card game?"

"We're gonna shoot the moon, Skyler Quinn," he promised with a charming wink. "We're gonna make room for sunrise and then watch it together."

The image made her smile. The image and the challenge. She remembered that shooting the moon meant collecting all the hearts in play, and this man clearly had the knack. But if there was one heart that wasn't going down on the table, it was hers.

So call your shots, cowboy. The night's as young as you are, and I'm game.

He lifted a strand of hair from her shoulder and rubbed it between his thumb and forefinger. "What do you call this color?"

"I think the bottle said strawberry."

"I don't see strawberries. I don't see a bottle. But I *have* seen this color somewhere." He abandoned her hair and took her hand, drawing her out of the booth. "It'll come to me."

"Where are we going?"

"To find some slow and easy holding-you-in-my-arms music. I just danced out of my twenties and I wanna dance into my thirties." He squeezed her hand. "You with me?"

"Yes, I am." She squeezed back. She was getting that giddy feeling again, and she was beginning to like it. "I like your style, cowboy."

"Skill takes you to the whistle, but it's style that wins the buckle."

Trace turned off the highway and followed a familiar dirt road to a spot overlooking the Powder River with a long view to the east. He'd found it back in his rookie days, and it was still a favorite place to pull off the highway and catch a little sleep knowing the sun would roust him in plenty of time to get to Casper to make the afternoon show and then head for

Denver or Boise. He slept just fine in the cab of his pickup as long as there were no headlights coming at him, no 18-wheelers whooshing past him in the night.

Skyler was asleep. At his suggestion, she'd cranked her seat back and drifted off in the middle of her own sentence. Something about not being able to sleep on the road. He wasn't going to let her sleep much longer. He'd flipped the center console upright and made way for a close encounter. With the moon on the run, it was the darkest part of a night that would soon be cracked by daylight. If he'd picked the right spot, they were in for a spectacular moment. But in the dark he couldn't be sure the landscape hadn't been sullied since his last visit. Miners and drillers were tearing into the Powder River country like some Biblical plague. He wanted this sunrise—his sunrise—to reveal nothing but pristine Wyoming.

But watching the woman sleep was nice, too. He was trying to decide how to wake her—whether to say her name or touch her bare shoulder, maybe her cheek—when she stirred, edging closer, giving faint voice to her soft sigh. He touched his lips briefly to hers and felt the sweet beginnings of a smile. He lifted his head and watched her lashes unveil her eyes, a gradual dawning. The smile vanished momentarily, but then it returned. It was too dark to see it in her eyes, but he knew it was there. He could feel the connection when she recognized him.

"Are we there yet?" she asked sleepily.

"No, but we're here. I promised you sunrise."

Her smile broadened as she closed her eyes. "I've seen it before."

"Not this one." The horizon was beginning to lighten. He released her seat belt and patted the empty leather space between them. "Come on over," he whispered, and he drew her under his arm as soon as she gave him the chance. She snuggled against him as though he were her favorite pillow. "Tell me about your mustang," he said. "How long have you had him?"

"Three weeks. I've managed to halter him, but that's about all."

"What do you want him to do for you?"

"Take me places."

"Where do you want to go?"

"I haven't decided. Maybe just down the road." She tipped her head back without lifting it from his shoulder. Out of the corner of his eye he saw her smile, and he felt favored and strangely honored by her ease with him. "Isn't that what you're doing, cowboy? Goin' down the road?"

He nodded. He wasn't feeling the *hell, yeah* he would have given with gusto back...when? A few months ago? A year? The rush that came with the ride was still good, but the road between rushes was getting longer. And something else, something that was beginning to wear on him more than sore muscles and aching joints. He wasn't ready to name it. Naming it would give it power, and he didn't feel like putting up a fight, not while this woman's head was resting on his shoulder. Which felt dangerously sweet.

"Here it comes." He laid his free hand on the top of the steering wheel and pointed a finger toward a burst of gold spearing through the pinks and purples washing over the jagged horizon. It was a common sight of incomparable beauty. "There it is, Skyler. On the edge of that cloud. I knew I'd seen that color before." He lifted a curl from her shoulder. "You have the morning sky in your hair."

"And you..." She sat up and looked him in the eye, laughing. "No, I won't say you have a silver tongue."

"I won't say don't knock it." He drew her close and she met his kiss fully, paying him back with interest, forcing him to be the reluctant quitter. "Mmm. That was a knockout."

"It surely was," she said dreamily. He liked the sound.

"And it's only day one."

"Between us we could cause a lot of damage in three days."

"Damage," he said as he touched her hair, "is not my style."

She gave him a quick *good boy* kiss and then turned her attention to the buoyant sun. "It's beautiful here," she said. But what he heard was *moving right along...* "This is the kind of place I want that mustang to take me."

"You picked the right trainer, then." He drew his arm over her head, effectively taking his pillow back. He was still thinking about those kisses. The first one was great. The second one rubbed him the wrong way. He knew what she was thinking.

Hell, he knew about a lot of things.

"Are you signed up with the Double D Wild Horse Sanctuary competition?"

"Mustang Sally's Makeover Challenge," she recited. He nodded, giving her pause. "You're not already in it, are you?"

"No, but my father is, and my brother was trying to get into it, too." He shrugged. *I'm way ahead of you, lady.* "I hear there's a big prize at stake."

A moment passed before she spoke again. "We have a deal, don't we?" From her tone, the shoe that had changed feet was a little tight. "The clock's already ticking on it."

He was a little surprised. He'd wanted her company, pure and simple, but he could have sworn her side of the deal was born of a whim. He didn't mind that her whim affected her need for his skill. She had already seen him make a difference with a horse and she'd soon realize there was more where that came from. Maybe there was more to this arrangement than he'd thought. Maybe there was more to this little dance of theirs, and maybe what had felt like a kiss-off was just a sweet little kiss.

And maybe she was a little more high maintenance

than he was used to, but, damn, he wasn't about to quit now.

He offered a smile. "Trust me, Skyler, I'm a man of my word."

"Trust *me*, cowboy, *trust me* is a line with a definite sell-by date." She raked her fingers through the hair he'd touched tenderly. "It expired for me a long time ago."

Don't ask, Wolf Track.

"Mike gave me the impression your husband was a good man."

That's asking, you idiot.

"He was." She sighed. "He was."

"If you don't wanna go back there, I sure don't mind moving ahead. It's a new day." *Right. Good luck with that.*

"The perfect beginning for a three-day event," she quipped. "You won't be competing against your family. I just need a little help getting over the first hump."

He made the catch, grinning and grateful. "Like I said, I'm your man."

"Briefly," she amended with a straight face, and he acknowledged with a shrug and a smile. "So let's make the most of it. I took this on thinking a horse is a horse."

"Of course."

"Of course!" Her laughter sounded girlish, and her eyes glittered in the morning sun like bits of green-

and-brown bottle glass. "But he's a wild horse, and he wanted absolutely no part of that halter."

"Yeah, but he wants a part of you," Trace said as he pulled the pickup keys out of the cup holder and plugged one into the ignition. "So he'll take the halter, the bit, the saddle, the whole crazy outfit," he continued as he put the pickup in gear. "Just give him free rein when you hit that next hump, and you'll go—" he made the jump with his hand, arching from gearshift to steering wheel "—up and over."

"Free rein," she echoed as she turned to him, her enthusiasm mounting as the pickup bumped and rattled over red clay ruts. "I saw a news clip about the competition and how they're trying to drum up support for the wild-horse sanctuary in South Dakota that those two sisters have devoted themselves to, put everything they have into it, and I just thought, this is important. I've trained horses. *I can do this.*" Her tone took a contemplative turn. "The wild ones are different, though. You wonder…"

"They're horses," he assured her.

"But they seem more sensitive. I swear, that horse can read my mind."

"That's a two-way street, isn't it?"

"Right now he isn't thinking *free rein*. He's thinking *no rein*."

"He can't imagine a rein, so go easy and try to stay one step ahead of him. You're just as sensitive as he is. You're a woman."

"Of course." She smiled playfully. "I know how to stay a step ahead without letting it show."

"There you go."

"Maybe I don't even need you."

"Maybe you don't, but you're curious about me." He returned her smile in kind. "It shows."

Curious didn't begin to describe where Skyler's head was. She was charmed, but she hoped it didn't show too much. She was as keyed up as a kid on her way to a carnival, but when he reminded her they'd be taking in the WYO Fair after he rode in his event, she tried to beg off, saying she didn't "do dizzy."

Trace was having none of it. No foot dragging today, he had said. It was a gorgeous midsummer day, and there was a program to get with, a crowd to entertain, a good time to be had. Skyler found herself eager to keep up with him, but something told her she'd better slow down, stay cool, be the grown-up. Childhood was, after all, much overrated.

Skyler had chosen to marry a man twice her age, and she'd worked hard to shed inconvenient youth in favor of sophistication. She'd achieved a certain dignity as Tony Quinn's wife for fifteen years and his widow for one. Dignity was about all she had left. She was too old to be a buckle bunny, too young to be a cougar and too smart to get herself stuffed, mounted and labeled with a trophy plaque. There wasn't a man in the big, wide world worth playing the fool for, not one.

Especially not one who regularly risked his fool neck bucking out rough stock. Skyler couldn't breathe watching Trace tether himself to a snorting sorrel bronc and call for the gate, but she couldn't close her eyes to the thrill of the horse's first jump and the skill of the man in making the jump his own. Trace rode the action more than the animal. He leaned back and became less the rider than the ride itself. He defined *going with the flow,* and it was breathtaking.

When the buzzer sounded, he bailed off the hurricane deck and landed on his feet. He waved his hat to the cheering crowd and then turned to where he'd left her, standing behind a chin-high fence under a Wrangler Jeans sign adjacent to the bucking chutes. Hat back in place, he dodged the pickup man, who was herding the high-stepping bronc toward the exit gate. Trace scaled the fence and swung over the top, but rather than drop to the ground, he eased himself rail by rail—giving her time to notice how nicely the fringed chaps framed the cowboy ass, Skyler supposed.

He turned and reached for her, and she stepped under his extended arm, slid her arms around his waist and gave him the kiss he deserved. Somebody sitting atop the chutes shouted, "Woo-hoo," and somebody else added, "Way to go, Trace!" He finished off the kiss with a little extra smooch and then gave the boys up top a wave with his free arm while he wheeled Skyler in the other direction, muttering something about his damn joints.

She tightened her hold on his side. "Are you okay?"

"Yeah, yeah. Just my trick knee." The smooth rowels on his spurs jingled as they rounded a fence corner and took refuge in an alley among the maze of stock pens. He flicked the chaps buckles loose at the back of his thighs, unbuckled the front and peeled them off.

"Can I help?"

"Thanks." He handed her the chaps, grabbed a rail with one hand and his knee with the other and "Sheee—" *Crack!* "—zam!" He straightened slowly. "Gotta start letting the pickup man do his job." He offered a sheepish grin. "Swear to God, that was my last flying dismount."

"It was magnificent," she enthused. "Can you walk?"

"Oh, yeah." He laid his arm around her shoulder and favored his knee as they walked. "All in an eight-second day's work."

"Won't it swell?"

"Not much. It's prewrapped. Did you get any good pictures?"

"I… No, I didn't. I forgot about the camera." She lifted the chaps she'd been clutching against her side. Yes, she still had her shoulder bag. "Oh my God, I forgot about the camera."

"You left it somewhere?"

"No, I have it. I was watching. I wasn't thinking

about anything else." He relieved her of the chaps and she smiled. "Pretty amazing."

"That watching can take your full attention?"

"That you can make a crazy ride like that look easy. The rest of those guys are working overtime, but you looked like you were quite comfortable. Like you were actually having fun."

"It's a helluvalot of fun when I'm on a roll. It's been a good season. Haven't broken anything in months."

"Ninety is a wonderful score. Do you think you'll win?"

"Can't lose." Grinning, he flipped the chaps over his shoulder. "It's my birthday."

"Let me take you out for dinner."

"You're on. I want a corn dog and a snow cone."

"I want to take you someplace nice."

"Exactly. The WYO Fair." He gave her a playful squeeze. "It's my *birthday,* woman! You take me to the corn-dog stand and I'll take you up on the Ferris wheel."

Skyler looked up. The wheel looked huge up close. The red seats rocked gently like the storied cradle in the treetops and the lights on the spokes were gaining on the dimming sky. She hadn't faced one of these things since Mike had last dragged her to a line like the one she was standing in now and handed off two tickets. She remembered being surprised that the top of his cowboy hat reached her nose, and he was barely eight.

She lowered her gaze and watched the cars dip, drag and rise. A starry-eyed young couple. Mom with kids. Dad with kids. Kids with kids. Lots of kids. Beautiful, beautiful kids. They all looked fairly secure, pretty happy. Begging off would have her looking like a stick-in-the-mud. It wasn't a roller coaster, after all. One Ferris wheel ride couldn't hurt.

"You wanna eat first?"

Skyler looked up at the handsome face below the brim of the cowboy hat. "Why don't we do this before we tackle the corn dogs?"

Going up was fine. Uploading. Uplifting. Upstanding. It was all good. At the top of the arc, she looked up at the sky, darkening from the top down as though an angel had bumped a bottle of blue ink. It washed over the remains of crimson and gold as the stars popped open one by one and hovered playfully just out of reach. Better than good, she thought.

"You won't find any prettier country than this," Trace said.

Skyler nodded. Her stomach signaled the shift from ascent to descent and her smile stiffened. She gripped the lap bar.

"You see that?" He laughed. "Guy just flew off the mechanical bull, landed on his head. Back to the bucking barrel for you, boy." He lifted his arm over her head and laid it across the back of the seat, glanced at her and then did a double take. "You okay?"

She nodded again. "Taller than I thought."

"Who, me?"

"The *thing*. The wheel. We're really high."

"Both of us? I was afraid it was just me. Gettin' hooked on a…" He paused, gave a look of concern and a blessed break. "Heights bother you?"

"A little."

"If you want me to, I can give the operator a distress signal when we hit bottom."

She shook her head. "No distress. Felt funny just because it was the first time around." She offered a tight smile. "You?"

"Yeah, a little." He snugged her up and she scooted a little closer as they slid across home plate and started back up. "Okay?"

"Talk to me. I don't want to be a wimp." But that was home. *Total ground control. Wimp city was a secure no-fly zone.* "My head says I'm fine, but some of my parts see it differently. I mean, my eyes are in my head, right? So how do my legs know how high up we are? And what's with my stomach?"

"It's probably talking to your legs, saying *get us off this thing.* How serious is it? What does your gut tell you? Because if it's saying—"

"It isn't. No rebellion in the making. It's just acting silly." She was looking up and out and feeling some improvement. But then came the lurch and the slow rocking, and she buried her face in his shirt. "Oh my God, we're stopping."

"Somebody's ride is over. We get down, yours will be, too."

"No, no, I have to do this." Head up, shoulders back. *Jennifer Grey in* Dirty Dancing. "I have to make the whistle."

"Nobody's scoring you, honey. You should've told me you don't like—"

"But I do. I mean, I *want* to. There's so much to see from here. I like this spot right here. As long as I keep my chin up, there's only up. Right?"

"Right. You want a score? Lean back, hang on to me. But not with this arm." He took her right hand from his shoulder and lifted it toward the sky. "That's your free arm. Can't touch this with that arm."

"Can't touch what?"

"Any of this." He referred to himself, hat to boots, with a sweep of his free hand. "You gotta control yourself in the face of the uncontrollable."

"Is this a twelve-step challenge?"

"Cowboy two-step, honey. We don't count much higher than that. Lean back and hang on."

She laughed.

"Not that we can't, but why bother? It doesn't get any better than two."

"Yes, it does. Two is just a start. Three is holy."

"Four is sacred."

"Seven is lucky."

"You are beautiful." He touched her chin and she

tipped her head to receive his kiss. A cool breeze lifted her hair while his warm kiss turned her sinking feeling into a rising one. "Feels like we're moving," she whispered against his lips.

"It does." He brushed her nose with his. "But we're not."

"Let's try again." She paid his kiss back, thinking to improve on it with his help. His fingers teasing her nape helped. His distracting tongue, his soothing breath, the pleasured sound coming from deep in his throat. "You're right," she said at last. "Two is just a start."

"If we count down from ten, I think we'll get lift-off." Another mechanical groan set the wheels in motion. She stiffened. He cuddled her close. "Hold me, Skyler."

"You'll deduct points."

"New rule," he said. "The more you touch, the better your score."

She laughed. "*You'll* get liftoff, and I'll be left hanging."

"I'm not goin' anywhere without you. Damn. We're moving."

"Distract me again."

She didn't have to ask twice. They kissed like teenagers who'd held off until the third date. She didn't care about numbers anymore—how many times around, how many birthdays, how many seconds, points, days, dollars or debts—she was deliriously distracted, disappointed when the ride slowed down and started unloading passengers.

"Mmm," she crooned. "I think we made it."

"Not even close." He winked at her as they came to their final stop. "But we will."

The ride operator—a clean-cut kid who might have been earning tuition money—grinned as Trace lifted his loop over Skyler's head. "I was about to apologize for the delay, but looks like you did okay with it."

"What delay?" she asked.

"Right after you guys got on we had to stop for a puking rider. You were probably stuck up top for a while, huh?"

Skyler looked at Trace. "Were we?"

He shrugged dramatically.

"You can keep going if you want. Otherwise—" the kid offered tickets "—next ride's on me."

"Thanks, but we're good. We're heading for the carousel." Trace waved the offer off. "We're horse people."

Chapter Three

"I was kidding about the snow cone."

But that was where they were heading. Skyler had the carnival midway's feedlot in her sights, and she was bearing down on a row of stands marked with painted fairgoer favorites, like an apple wearing a caramel coat and bananas splashing around in a vat of chocolate.

"I was actually looking forward to the corn dog," she said merrily as she turned and let him catch up. "A rare treat, as it should be but still…" She folded her arms and took a Mama stance, but the look in her eyes was all about big flavor, little nutrition. "Perfect for a kid's birthday party."

"You kiddin' me, woman? What kid?" Without pausing he hooked his arm around her and swept her along, zeroing in on a fading picture of two dancing corn dogs. "Do I kiss like a kid?"

"Uh-uh."

"Uh-uh. And I'm not the one who wimped out on the Ferris wheel. Sure, I like playing games, but my game pays pretty well." He lined them up for supper on a stick. "When I'm on my game. 'Course, as of today, I'm past my prime. Over the hill." He flashed the ponytailed man in the window a two-fingered order. "Are you a mustard or ketchup girl?"

"I like mine unsauced." She took the deep-fried dog in hand and flashed him a *yum-yum* smile. "Clean and sober."

"Hold mine, then." He chuckled as he pumped mustard from a gallon jug into a small paper cup. "Down and dirty."

They finished their main course in silence, eyeing pictures of their follow-up options as they strolled amid parents catering to children and couples caught up in each other. It was a good time to be part of a pair. Trace didn't always feel that way, but tonight was different. It was his birthday and he was with somebody. Not just hanging out, but being together and actually looking forward to another day of the same.

Without the birthday, of course. So maybe not quite the same. Or maybe better. He damn sure wanted to find out whether he'd like her even more tomorrow.

"Last I heard, the hill was forty. Not that I've been

there myself." She gave him the over-to-you eye as they tossed their wooden sticks in a red trash bin.

"What?" He wasn't going there either.

"Go ahead and ask."

"I was raised by a gentleman." To prove it he offered his arm. She smiled, tucked her hand in the crook of his elbow and they walked on. "Let me ask you this—how old was Mike when you married his dad?"

"He was seven. I took a summer job as his nanny. I was—" she glanced up at him, her eyes teasing "—in college. I didn't finish." She lifted one shoulder. "Unfortunately."

"Me neither. The only subject I was interested in at the time was college rodeo. But I don't say it was unfortunate. I say, fortunately I can go back when I'm ready." He tuned in to the distant echo of the rodeo announcer talking up the final event. Bull riding. Unless a buddy was entered up, Trace didn't care to stick around for the grand finale. "I was ten when Logan came along," he went on. "It's never too late for good fortune."

"Or snow cones," Skyler said cheerfully as she dragged her boot heels to a halt. He followed her gaze to the top of a tiny stand. Big Bad Ice.

"You want one?" Matching her delight, his cool was blown.

"No." She went from straight face to sassy smile. "But I'll have some cotton candy."

He let her taste his purple snow cone and she fed

him wisps of spun pink sugar. They shared a deep-fried funnel cake and a crisp cone full of frozen custard. She sang "Happy Birthday" to him over the cake and he smiled at the way her tongue stormed that tower of custard, her green eyes flashing as she left no surface unlicked. He pointed to the drip at the point of the cone and she caught it before it escaped and then sucked noisily for good measure.

She caught him staring.

"Your turn." She lifted the tongue-marked treat close to his mouth. "Sorry, but it's melting so fast and it's the kind that needs licking."

"I know the feeling."

"Well, we've already exchanged..." she said, as Trace plunged the tip of his tongue into custard, curled it and scooped out a substantial niche. "Oh."

"Don't give me that look. It was my turn." He licked his lips as he scanned new midway territory. "You like to play games, too, don't you?"

"That's what birthdays are all about. Fun and games." She handed him the rest of the ice cream, lighting up as she pointed at a new attraction. "Ring-toss! Now we're talking." And she was walking off on him again. She had the prettiest, most purposeful stride he'd seen on a woman, and her jeans loved her for it.

But his knee didn't. He did a little hop-step as he followed her to a stand that housed an arrangement of bottles and an array of stuffed toys.

"Slow down, honey, you've got an injured man here."

She turned in front of the stand, smiling and giving him the come-on as if nobody was hurting. "I'm gonna win you a birthday present."

"It's your birthday?" the burly huckster asked as he spread three plastic rings on the counter. "First toss is on the house, then. Happy birthday, cowboy."

"Getting older *and* better," Skyler reported as she reached into her purse. "He gave a fearless performance a while ago."

"Let me guess," the man said. "Bronc rider."

"That, too," she quipped. Trace laughed, elbowing her as he slapped some cash on the counter. She snatched it up ahead of the ringtoss man and tucked it under the flap of his Western-style shirt pocket. "Pick your prize, and it's yours."

He smiled into her eyes. "I only see one thing I want, and I'll have to win that myself."

"The sky's the limit."

"Then I'm all in."

"And I'm all ears, waitin' to hear who's payin'," said the huckster. "Sounds like the lady's landed her share of rings."

Trace warned the man with a look—the lady was in no way his business—and then glanced at the next booth. "How are you at knocking down milk bottles?"

"This is *my* game. Really. It doesn't pay well, but I'm very good at lots of things that don't pay well."

She traded cash for plastic rings and then she sized up the targets. "What should I go for?"

"A rabbit's foot." He gave a nod. "That pink one."

"That's too easy. Pick a top-row prize." She pointed to the big stuffed bunny.

"I'd look pretty silly carrying around a pink rabbit. All I want is the foot."

"Come on, cowboy. I like a challenge as much as the next person."

"Good to know." He gave her a little smile. "I've got two more days to come up with one that isn't rigged."

"Hey, this game ain't—"

Huckster took the hint. He folded his arms over his man boobs and watched his pints and quarts.

Skyler hit one of each, and Trace gave an appreciative whistle.

"It doesn't matter whether it's rigged," she told him as she lined up her next shot. "It's all in the wrist."

Skyler won the rabbit's foot in three tosses. "Three ringers, zero misses. The big three-o." She held her hand out for the chosen prize, which the huckster quickly turned over. She slid it into Trace's shirt pocket with his money. "Very lucky, indeed."

He lifted his pocket flap and eyed his present. "Not according to a certain pink rabbit hopping around somewhere on three legs."

Trace didn't want his day to end, but it was almost midnight. The lights of Sheridan glimmered beyond the last intimate stretch of darkness. They'd traveled a long, quiet road, and he'd taken it slow and easy.

"You must be tired," she said, breaking a remarkably comfortable silence. "You have to ride again tomorrow night, don't you?"

"One more go-round. I'm sittin' first right now, so, yeah, I should catch a little sleep." He glanced at her and smiled. "But I'm sorry to see the day end."

"You had a good birthday?"

"The best. I was gonna let it come and go like I usually do, but you came along and changed things. Change is good."

"Not always."

"It was good for me." The headlights illuminated a city-limits sign, and he eased up on the gas. "I'll make it good for you, too. You've got two days coming."

"Wow. I might have to rethink my plan."

"You do that." He nodded. "And then I'll do what I do best."

"Your end of the bargain starts *after* the rodeo." She chuckled. "Do you realize how many times eight seconds goes into two days?"

"I'm only signed up for one timed event. Everything else is off the clock."

"So my two days won't start until—"

"Not until I can give you my undivided attention. One more ride." He patted his shirt pocket. "Try out my new rabbit's foot. Oh, and I have tickets for you. Best seats in the house. You and Mike."

"Mike is going home today. At least, he said he

would. Right after the slack events. He has work to do. We have a hired man who needs to be kept busy."

"Must be hard. Losing his father is bad enough, but picking up the slack on the ranch, young as he is…" Another sign appeared in the headlights. They were back at the hotel. Trace slowed the pickup. The turn signal sounded like a grandfather clock echoing down a long hallway. "The man of the house, he said. Sounded like a line from a movie."

"He said that?" Skyler laughed. "A line from a movie describes it perfectly. But the only place it's playing is in Mike's head."

"So…no other kids?"

"No other kids. Michael is all he…all *we* had."

"Why does he call you by your first name?"

She lifted one shoulder. "I asked him if he wanted to call me Mom, and his only answer was to keep calling me Skyler. He's never had any problem letting me take care of him, but I was never quite Mom."

"He said you were his mother." Trace raised his brow, giving his recollection a second thought. "Then he said *step*mother."

"And that's *correct,* isn't it? Technically. *Legally,* even though I'm the one who's been there. Maybe he thought his father made all the decisions for both of us because for a long time he did. The big ones, anyway. But we never talked about adoption." She gave a perfunctory smile. "It doesn't matter what he calls me. He's my son."

"He's a nice guy." Trace turned off the motor. He'd passed several parking spaces close to the front entrance and chose one at the far end of the lot before he turned to her.

Here it comes, she thought. *The big move.*

"He'll grow into those boots," Trace said.

Meaning he wasn't ready, either. Or maybe he wasn't as interested as she'd thought. Assumed. *Hoped?*

She'd been mentally vacillating among possible responses to probable approaches like *How about a drink?* And *My room or yours?* Unoriginal propositions—he was a cowboy, after all—could be refused easily enough if she wasn't, for some foolish reason, hoping for something. But what? Something quick and easy that would move her off dead center? This night couldn't amount to much more than that. Not with a rodeo cowboy.

"Mike got interested in rodeo when he was in high school," she told him, surprised at how easy it was to kick an expectation aside, especially when it was open-ended. "About the time his father's health started to decline. Tony had always been a pretty good roper, but he gave it up after his first stroke. Mike got him into team penning, which was good for both of them. And Tony's outlook improved when Mike tried calf roping."

She glanced through the windshield, into the night. "Then Tony had another stroke, and he just couldn't…get back in the saddle, you might say. It was hard for Mike to watch his father break down, piece by piece."

"Must have been hard on you."

"Hard on me?" She shrugged. "I did what I had to do. Mike never had to do much, so he watched. Until he couldn't anymore and then he found more and more reasons to stay away."

"You're a strong woman."

"He was my husband. And Mike is..." She gave him a smile. Wistful. *Grateful.* "Michael is Michael."

"Well, he picked himself a decent prospect. Got himself a hell of a trainer, so now he has a fine horse under him, and he just needs to throw that rope every chance he gets and pick up his groundwork." He nodded. "Mike made a good catch yesterday. A few like that could start the fire in his belly."

"Is that what makes you do it? Fire in the belly?"

"A guy's gotta eat."

"I've seen how you eat. The fire in your belly might be from junk food."

"I've seen how *you* eat," he teased. "Watching you go after that ice cream was...stimulating."

"That was no ice cream, cowboy. It was frozen custard. Soft serve."

"For you, maybe." He gave her one of those cocky winks of his and let himself out of the pickup.

Skyler followed suit. *Was that it?* Granted, she hadn't thought about the dating game in years, wasn't even sure what they called it these days, but had she lost her knack for reading the opposite sex? Trace was going to bed, where he meant to sleep.

"I'm gonna take another look at that horse I tried out when you were taking pictures," he said when he came around to her side of the pickup. "I'd like to get your opinion."

"You would?"

"Yeah. You put him through his paces and tell me what you think." He pushed his hat back and briefly rubbed the bandage on his forehead. "After we eat. A good meal this time. Birthday party's over."

"I really enjoyed it, Trace. You've got the right idea. For one whole day, just say yes." She glanced up, offered a *poor baby* look. "How's the head?"

"Hat's a little tight. When's *your* birthday?"

"Not telling."

"Come on. I'll bring all the junk food." He took her shoulders in his hands. "Call me when you're ready for breakfast. We'll pick up where we left off."

"Which was?"

"Here." He lowered his head for a kiss, and they made it the kind they both regretted leaving off.

By midmorning, the hotel lobby was quiet except for the woman arguing over her bill with the desk clerk while her husband shushed the two young children who wanted food. The boy was also trying to talk his little sister out of a stuffed alligator exactly like one Skyler had seen at the ringtoss booth, but the girl had a choke hold on the gator and was having none of her brother's pathetic offers. Her pigtails bobbled each time she shook her head. She laughed when he made a face at her, which prompted him to repeat his woeful claim that he was starving and his sister to chime in with "Me, too, me, too, me, too."

One child would be enough, Skyler told herself as she closed the horse magazine she'd been thumbing through. Girl or boy. She'd feed her on time, and she wouldn't have her stand there watching her mother argue about two phone calls and a bag of peanuts. The boy was probably about seven or eight. They could be a handful at that age. Boys could be a handful at any age. *Maybe a girl,* Skyler thought. *A daughter.* It was just a *what if,* she reminded herself as the child glanced at her suddenly. Sensitive little beings, weren't they? Skyler smiled, and the little girl smiled back.

"Hey, Skyler, where were you yesterday?"

Skyler turned to the sound of Mike's voice as he emerged from the dim first-floor hallway.

"Were you looking for me?"

"I thought maybe you'd caught a ride back home. Tried calling, but…" He took the leather-bound chair kitty-corner from hers and leaned in to offer his most endearing smile. "You still mad?"

"About what?" If she were, they both knew it wouldn't last long. That boyish look of his always got to her.

"You know. Setting you up with Earl."

"Is that all you did?" She shook her head. "I know you meant well, Mike, but don't. Okay? Just don't."

"You've been hangin' back long enough. I know you're not ready to jump off the high dive, so I thought we'd ease you into the shallow end, you know?"

"Poor Earl. The stationary horse on the dating merry-go-round."

She slid a furtive glance toward the restaurant. If she was getting stood up, she probably deserved it, considering poor Earl. Rather than call and wake him up, she'd left a message telling Trace she'd gone downstairs for coffee. As if she had her own agenda, but she'd made room for him if he was still interested.

"That's cold," Mike was saying.

"So is the shallow end of the pool, Mike. It's cold and it's boring. I'm only interested in strong swimmers, and you don't find many of those at three feet."

"Of course not. You gotta go six, at least. Dad was over six feet."

"The answer is no, I'm not mad at you." She let his six-foot illusion pass. She remembered a time when she'd shared it. She hadn't been much older than Mike was now and Tony Quinn was the man in charge.

"Good," he said. "What time do you want to take off?"

"I think I'm staying for the rodeo tonight."

"Even better! I just talked to Grady. He wants

to knock that alfalfa down a little earlier than we planned so we can get ahead of the weevils. But one or two more days won't... Wait a minute." His delight turned to disbelief. *"Trace Wolf Track?"*

"What?"

"You're with Trace?"

"The high dive is out of the question, Michael. I'm afraid of heights." Skyler failed to suppress a smile. "Last I rode the Ferris wheel."

"You mean you...you and Trace?" He looked like a kid who'd just realized that his mama *did* dance.

"I mean I *rode a Ferris wheel.* We went to Casper."

"For the rodeo," he filled in.

"And the fair. Corn dogs, cotton candy, frozen custard, ringtoss. I won a prize." She patted Mike's knee. "So I want you to go home and get ahead of the weevils. Trace is going to take me home and he's going to help me with the mustang."

"You were pissed when I gave you his bill for training Bit-o-Honey."

"We're trading services." She spread her hand over the picture of *The Quarter Horse* on her lap. "I've been taking lots of pictures and most of them are actually pretty good. Trace says he'll get me closer to the action tonight. I know how to get those human-interest moments behind the scenes, but I want to work on getting good action shots, especially out-doors, even under the lights. That's where it gets tricky. Trace won't be riding under the lights, but by the time they get around to saddle bronc…"

His eyes glazed over. "I don't know, Skyler. Rodeo photography is kinda specialized."

"I'm exploring," she said. "I know I can sell more pictures. I just need to broaden my horizons. Function the way the horse does. Diversify."

"I think it's great, you getting out there, but you wanna watch out for those—"

"Hey, Mike." Skyler looked up to find Trace towering over her behind her chair. He met her startled glance with *you and me* in his eyes as he touched her shoulder and mouthed *morning* before turning back to Mike. "How'd you do yesterday?"

"I, uh…didn't qualify for the final round, but Bit-o-Honey sure did his job." Mike stood up, and Skyler followed in the next heartbeat. "How 'bout you? Hear you went down to Casper."

"I made the whistle."

"He won," Skyler reported happily. "And I realized—you know, from a photographer's perspective—there's so much that goes into that eight-second ride that you don't see unless you…" The amusement in Trace's eyes didn't escape her. She smiled back at him. *That's right. I forgot about the camera.* "Well, unless you're up close and personal."

"You mean, like the woman trying to knock the cowboy's teeth out with her microphone?" Mike substituted his fist in a mock interview. "Talk about how it feels, Trace."

Skyler dropped her voice and added a twang. "Feels like hell, but it smells like victory."

"There's none of that kind of coverage in Casper." Trace nodded at Skyler. "I don't sound like that, but it's a great line. Mind if I use it?"

"It's all yours."

"So..." Mike shifted and shuffled, but nobody was looking. "I guess I'll be heading back to do some honest work. Nothing like finishing out of the money to take the cowboy out of the cattleman."

"From what I hear, not too many cattlemen are finishing in the money these days, either," Trace said.

"Skyler says we gotta diversify."

"Sounds like good advice for all of us."

"But you've got nothing to worry about, Trace," Mike said. "You always find your way to the pay window."

"Not always. Show me a cowboy with nothing to worry about, I'll show you a man with a backup plan."

"Hell, what cowboy do you know has a Plan B?" Mike laughed. "Unless B is for buckle."

"No, that's Plan A," Trace said. "You go home and study your letters, boy. You get down to C, that's when you cowboy up."

"And then D-versify," Skyler said. She was enjoying this. Mike didn't quite know what to think of the fact that his friend was suddenly her friend.

"It's good to see you having some fun," he said to Skyler.

"I have no idea what he's talking about," Skyler said as she watched Mike push through the glass entrance doors. "I'm always having fun. Even when I'm working I'm having fun." She turned to find Trace smiling at her, as though he got a kick out of watching her protest too much. "But not this much fun."

"How much?"

"Enough to make me change my plans and stay another day. That's huge."

"Were you planning something huge?"

"I was planning to stick with the plan I made before I ran into you," she told him as they headed for the hotel restaurant. "It's the *change* that's huge. Anything else has yet to be seen."

"Honey, the fun has just begun."

Two hours later, Trace watched Skyler ride the sorrel roping horse he'd tried out two days ago under the watchful eye of her camera lens. Only two days? He'd been thinking about the woman so much, he'd almost forgotten about the horse. But watching the gelding move beneath Skyler—who made every move look as though it was all the horse's idea—made him want both.

He didn't want Skyler watching him dicker with the horse's owner over a price—couldn't afford to have her cramping his horse-trading style—so he signaled her for another turn around the arena while he closed the deal. He didn't mind taking advantage of the fact that the owner wanted to unload the horse so he could buy a better one. This time next year Trace would be considering the "better" one. A horse would only do so much for a rider who was all muscle and no finesse.

Trace knew the makings of a profit when he saw it, but that wasn't the side of his business he liked to display. Not to someone like Skyler. He wanted to show her what a horse would do for Trace Wolf Track, and he wanted to show her how he got there, from start to finish.

With the deal in his pocket and the sorrel fed and watered, Trace took Skyler behind the chutes and introduced her to some of his competitors. No one refused her request for pictures, and she offered printed cards to direct them to her online photo display and promised to send them prints of anything they liked. Then she stepped back and quietly snapped pictures of riders with wives, girlfriends, kids and other cowboys while Trace made sure his gear was in order, his body loosened up and his mind tightly focused.

Some cowboys donned parade chaps for the Grand Entry, but bareback was first on the program, so Trace didn't have to participate in the preliminaries. Like all athletes, he had his pregame rituals, but hanging over the chutes and tensing up wasn't one of them. It was Trace's custom to get ready, get set and then let go. He wasn't going to count down the minutes or worry about the darkening sky.

He tore Skyler away from the rodeo's staging area, found her a vantage point above the chutes where they could watch the stock handlers sort out the bareback horses and move them through the gates.

"That's my ride, that sleepy-looking dun over there." He pointed out the calmest horse in the first bunch. "Look at him, pretending he doesn't care what's going down. We've got a history, Vegas and me."

"Doesn't look like you'd be taking much of a gamble on him."

"He's a sure bet if you can stick him. That sleepy look is a con. They call him Vegas because he's a high roller. Comes alive as soon as the gate opens. Jumps up real pretty when he's in the mood. Snakier'n hell when he's not. Either way, he's a good draw." He allowed himself one quick look skyward. "Just hope it don't rain."

"Oh, but think of the pictures." She tucked her arm around his elbow. "I'd love a good splatter shot."

"And I thought you were my friend."

"I am. I'll gladly take on a share of the mud if you'll get me inside."

"Inside?"

"The arena. Can't I get inside the fence?"

"You got a card?"

She questioned him with a frown.

"I can get you behind the chutes, but you gotta be a card-carryin' Professional Rodeo Cowboy Association photographer to get inside the arena." He wagged a finger against whatever retort was about to come from those pretty lips. "For good reason. The rider has no control over the animal. You're on your own and so is everybody on the ground."

"I have a good zoom, but I like to be able to maneuver."

"So does Vegas." He wiped a drop of rain off her cheek with his forefinger. "Looks like you'll get your splatter shot."

"Or maybe you'll get rained out."

"This ain't no baseball game, honey. I don't get paid unless I ride."

But the sky wasn't fooling. Scattered drops turned into a deluge just as they reached Trace's pickup parked in the contestants' lot near the stock pens. Trace jerked the passenger door open and ducked inside the cab behind Skyler, both of them laughing.

"What happens now?"

She was looking up at him, all wide-eyed and eager, as though he had a hat full of magic. He had to take it off and check. He chuckled as he tossed it on the backseat. A bloodstain on the brow band didn't count.

"Now we watch it rain," he said with a sigh. "And maybe we talk and I start thinking about my last ride in a muddy arena."

"What happened?"

He lifted his arm over her head and put it around her shoulders. "Or we make out like two horny teenagers who don't have a care in the world except getting pregnant." He lifted her chin and kissed her softly. "Which means we enjoy the hell out of first and second bases."

She smiled, her eyes all dewy. "This ain't no baseball game, honey."

"And we're not teenagers."

"We're responsible adults," she whispered.

"Careful what you pitch me, woman. I can read your signals." He slid his fingers across her back. "Must be a clasp here somewhere."

"You talk too much, cowboy." She buried her fingers in his hair and pulled his head down for a base-stealing kiss.

A five-minute rain led them into temptation, and foggy windows delivered them from gawkers. She opened herself to him—her arms, her mouth, her sensitivity to every shift or sound or silent supplication—and it was all he could do to contain himself.

"Bareback riders, report to the chutes," called the announcer.

Damn those wimpy rain clouds.

Back-to-back, she fiddled with her camera while he fooled with his rigging. Maybe Trace carried the momentum from one kind of rush to the next, but Skyler needed a little Zen stillness to move her from the *life* side of the mirror to the *art* side. *Inhale slowly. Exhale. Steady, Skyler, he's only a man.*

But he was focused. The line *He spoke not a word, but went straight to his work* came to mind as she claimed the vantage he'd suggested—halfway up the fence adjacent to the bucking chutes. From there she photographed his every preparatory move—checking the cinch, taking his seat, taking his grip, pounding his gloved hand to set the rosin on the rigging grip and finally grabbing a piece of sky with his free hand and calling for the gate.

Skyler's heart pogoed into her throat, but she would not miss those action shots this time. The bronc sprang free of the chute like a flying reindeer. Trace marked his horse out—spurs above the shoulders—and took the first jump in classic bareback-rider style—back-to-back and spurs to shoulders. The front hooves' first landing gave Skyler the coveted splatter shot. His chaps flapped like fringed bat wings as he racked up the points by spurring high, wide and handsome. Skyler tried to forget who he was so she could remember to keep him centered in her viewfinder. She wondered how much punishment his riding arm could take. Without bit, reins or saddle, the only part of the ride he could control was his body. He had the strength and skill of a gymnast or a trapeze artist, except that his apparatus had muscle and mind of its own.

Four Mississippi, five Mississippi... She wasn't breathing. She wondered whether he was. *...six ride him, cowboy, seven one more second... Bzzzz!*

He made the whistle, but he missed the pickup rider and down he went.

Skyler froze.

A clown and a cowboy wearing an official Justin Sportsmedicine Team vest pulled Trace out of the mud while the second pickup man released Vegas's flank strap, and the high-headed horse cantered toward the exit as if to say, *Step aside, boys. My work here is done.*

Trace was on his feet, but only one leg was steady. Between clown and cowboy medic he left the arena through the gate instead of the preferred over-the-fence exit. But the crowd cheered him—first for his plucky wave and then for his high score. The open gate gave Skyler several clear camera shots.

"Comin' through," the clown barked, and Trace didn't look at her. A tall Indian cowboy took over for the clown, who scowled at Skyler as he passed on his way back to the arena. Clearly, she'd committed some offense.

She shoved her camera into her bag and followed Trace and his human crutches to the medical tent, where she was able to talk herself inside. He was the evening's first casualty, so he had the no-nonsense medical team's full attention. A big, tail-wagging yellow dog was part of the reception crew.

"Who're you?" a woman in a pink shirt demanded. She had the Sportsmedicine patch on her sleeve. She was official.

"Skyler," Trace called out. "She's with me."

Somebody piped up behind her. "You trust her with your hat, Trace?"

"Damn straight." He acknowledged her with a glance and a nod, but he was concentrating on keeping upright while the aides peeled off his muddy chaps. They hoisted him up on an exam table. "How'd you do?" he asked Skyler.

"How did *I* do?" Somebody tapped her arm from behind and "trusted" her with a muddy cowboy hat as she edged closer. Absently fingering the brim, she watched the medical team handle their charge with care. "Is it your knee?" she asked.

"Ankle. Mostly." Trace was looking up at one of the men who'd brought him this far—tall, attractive, vaguely familiar Indian cowboy, who she now noticed wore the red-and-black Justin Sportsmedicine patch on the sleeve of his crisp white, once clean Western shirt.

Where had she seen him before?

"Did you get your pictures this time?" Trace was asking.

"I think so." She watched the medic bend to the task of removing Trace's boot. "How bad is it?" she asked gently.

"Ahh!" Trace gripped the edge of the exam table. The dog nosed his hand until he relaxed it and petted her big shiny head. "Just cut it off, Hank."

"Aw, c'mon, it can't be *that* swollen yet. These boots look barely broke in. Hang on, it's comin'."

"Ah!" The boot came off in the medic's strong hands followed by a brown sock. "Damn, that smarts. It ain't broke. Look, I can—ahh! But I can move it just fine." The dog whimpered and licked Trace's toes.

"He's okay, Phoebe," the medic said. "Can you feel that?"

"Yeah." Trace braced himself on his arms and leaned back. "Wet, warm and gentle."

"Best nurse around." The medic rolled up the bottom of Trace's jeans. "What about the knee?"

"No problem. Skyler was just takin' a wild guess." He flashed a tight smile over the medic's head. "Skyler, you know Hank Night Horse?"

"I don't… You look familiar." The man spared her a glance and a chance, but his name wasn't ringing any bells. "Skyler Quinn," she offered. "How bad is it?"

"If Trace says it ain't broke, there's nothing to fix." He took Trace's ankle in hand.

"What do *you* say?" she asked.

"Nothing yet. He just got here." The medic was intent on his examination. "You want an X-ray, Trace?"

"No."

"Good, 'cause I left my Superman cape back at the Double D. I can send you to the E.R., but…" He pressed gently while he slowly rotated Trace's foot. "Wiggle your pigs."

Trace moved his toes. "I can do that all the way home."

"As long as you're not driving. It's swellin' up pretty good, but I don't think anything's broken. You'll know soon enough if you've got a fracture. Short of that, you know what to do. Gen, could you get us some—" the woman in the pink shirt plunked a plastic bundle in the medic's outstretched hand "—cushion?"

"Right." She snatched a vinyl-covered cushion off an empty exam table. "You were thinking ice, Hank." She turned away muttering, "Best nurse around, he says."

"You want Gen to shave you, Trace? She needs a job."

"Hell, no. Use the underwrap," Trace said.

"Keep your ol' leg hair, then," Gen said and Trace laughed.

Skyler was thinking Double D, the wild horse sanctuary, the competition. "That's where I saw you," she told the medic. "You're the farrier."

"Feet are my specialty." He had Trace's propped up, and he was applying the ice. "Lie back and take it easy," he told Trace. "You've won yourself a roll of tape."

"Better be more than that." Trace finally gave in and lay back. "Heard you got hitched, Doc."

"Sure did. Your dad and me, both. Where the hell were you?"

"On the road." Trace laughed. "Hell, if I'd known it was you and Logan, I wouldn't've missed it. Must've been a pretty sight. Who carried the flowers?"

"Sally and Mary did, you smart-ass. You wouldn't wanna piss me off while you're on my table, Wolf Track."

"Not Sally *Drexler*," Skyler said.

"Not anymore," Hank said with a proud smile. "She goes by Sally Night Horse now."

"I love what she's doing with her ranch, turning

it into a home where the wild horse roams," Skyler said. "I entered the mustang training competition."

Hank nodded. "How's the horse coming along?"

"Slowly. Trace was going to give me a few pointers. But now…"

"He can still point." Hank pulled out a length of stretchy white tape and started a figure-eight wrapping. "Baby him for twenty-four hours or so, and then make him start putting some weight on it. If he can't, he gets it x-rayed."

"Hey," Trace said. "It's my ankle."

"What, you're not gonna milk it?" Hank cut the tape, tossed it in a box and took out a roll of green tape and another of red.

"Trace Wolf Track in here?" The cowboy clown stuck his head in the tent door, looked around and snapped one of his red suspenders when he located his target. "Hey, man, you took first in bareback. They want me to get you out there for the announcement."

"They love a wounded winner," Hank said. "Load him up on the go-cart and let him take his bow."

"I'll take my check," Trace muttered as he sat up.

"I'll get him a walking cast boot," Gen said. "Stay out of the mud with it, though."

"I ain't finished with him, so don't let him out of the cart." Hank smiled at Skyler. "Like they say, the show must go on."

Chapter Four

Armed with crutches, ice pack and pills, Trace turned his keys over to Skyler and climbed into the passenger's side of his pickup. From the swelling and the kind of pain Trace was experiencing, Hank had suspected at least a second-stage sprain and loaded him down with warnings. The crowd's adulation had cheered him, and collecting his check had taken that up a notch, but Skyler had a feeling the man would crash soon and she didn't feel like driving a hundred miles tonight.

She started the pickup and turned to him. "Let's get you to bed."

"You say that like you think you're gonna tuck me in and kiss me good-night." He slid down in the seat and offered a slow, sexy grin. "Take another look and think again."

She had no idea what that was supposed to mean. The party was over. The less damaged cowboys would be heading for the next rodeo. "You heard the man. He said *elevate*."

"Hell, I got no problem elevating. I am…" True to his name, his hazel eyes glittered. "Let's get *you* to bed."

"At least I don't have to ask what kind of drugs you're on."

"El-ev-ate! El-ev-ate!" he sang as she turned the pickup onto a hill.

She had to laugh. "I'm glad you're feeling no pain. Once we get you down, you will be out."

"That's why I ain't goin' down, darlin'. I already checked out."

"I did, too, but we can check back in. You're—"

"Win or lose, I ain't payin' for another night. I told you I was leaving after the rodeo, and you said you were going with me."

"There's been a slight change in the plan, cowboy."

"Another change? Damn, that came easy."

"We've already agreed. Change is good."

He dropped his head back and smiled at the ceiling. "Yeah, but this one won't be slight."

"We'd have to go back to the rodeo grounds and find your trailer. You did bring a horse trailer."

"Never leave home without it."

"I'd have to hitch it up. I'd have to load your new horse." She glanced at him. So far he wasn't taking exception. "And since my place is on the way to yours, you'd have to lay over for a while."

He turned his silly smile on her. "Lay over who?"

"You're incorrigible."

"Ha! You love it."

"And you're all alike."

"All who?" He waved her answer off. "Nah, forget it. Just tell me when I'm like nobody else. Whisper it in my ear. *You're different, Trace. I've never met anyone like you, Trace.*" His smile mellowed. "Because you're already there, Skyler. You're like nobody else."

"You hardly know me."

"You're hard to know. Mmm, but you're so very easy to look at."

"Thank you."

They'd reached the hotel. She parked close to the side entrance, got out of the pickup, went around to the passenger's side and opened the door.

He didn't move. "What are we doing here?"

"They're holding my bag at the desk."

"Oh, yeah, let me get that for you." He sat up, grabbed the door and swung himself onto the pavement, one leg jacked up like a flamingo.

"It's on wheels. What do you need out of the back?"

"Nothing." He patted the front pocket of his jeans. "Got my spare foot right here. The pink one."

"Besides ice pack, crutches—" she opened the back door of the crew cab and found the first two items "—toothbrush, pajamas."

"*Pajamas!* Good luck with that, woman."

She positioned his crutches and he flapped his wings. "Good luck with that, cowboy. I'd let you lean on me, but you seem a little buzzed. I'm afraid we'd both go down."

He moved one crutch and hopped a couple of inches. "These damn sticks don't fit me."

They really weren't a bad fit, but he gave her such a befuddled look that she wasn't going to argue. Back into the backseat went the crutches. She drew his arm around her shoulders and told him it wasn't far. "You stayed on that crazy horse, and now you're gonna let a pair of crutches throw you?"

"Nope. I'm stayin' off 'em. You ever ride a stick horse?"

"Probably."

"Neither did I. Never had one. I wanted one, but I never got it."

"Step up," she told him at the door. She noticed he didn't put any extra weight on her when he hopped up the single step. *Big faker.* But it took them a while to get to the lobby, which was quiet. She breathed a sigh of relief when they reached a chair.

"I'm a lightweight when it comes to painkillers."

"I wouldn't say that. Sit. Take a load off both of

us." She bent to lift his bandaged foot and place it on the coffee table. She glanced up when he thanked her. He smiled dreamily.

She came back with her wheeled bag in tow and offered him a hand. "We're on the first floor. No stairs."

"I never stay in town once the rodeo's over."

"But there's only one bed."

He took her hand. "Like I said, it sure would be nice to lie down and elevate."

It was an old hotel, and the room was small but nicely appointed with a brass bed, a highboy and a vanity. Trace said he was too dirty to sit on the bed, so she helped him to the low-back wooden chair, stood back and took a look at him in the soft light.

"You need food," she determined.

"I need a shower more than anything." He glanced around the room. "*Almost* anything. I could use a shot of Jack Daniel's."

"*Food.* I'll order something, and then I'll get your stuff from the pickup." She glanced at his booted foot. "Where would I find you some clothes?"

"There's a duffel bag in the back and a pair of Ariats on the floor. My favorite boots. They lace up."

"Perfect," she said, genuinely cheered by that news. But then she considered the taped foot. "I don't know how you'll manage in the shower."

"I don't, either. Probably need some help."

"Does it still hurt?"

"Like a sonuvabitch." She gave him a doubtful look and he smiled. "You wouldn't know it, though, would you? I'm toughin' it out."

"I'm impressed." Back to the bandaged foot. "You can't get that wet."

"You think?"

"So I don't know how you'll manage." She shook her head sadly. "Keep on toughin', I guess."

He burst out laughing.

"What do you want to eat?"

"Not much." He started up from the chair, and she went to his side. "I'm good," he told her. "Plenty of wall to hang on to."

"And a safety rail in the shower."

"Yeah, they think of everything these days."

"Still, there's that bandage…"

He slipped his arm over her shoulder. "Truth is, that bandage ain't goin' nowhere. Hank's a master taper and a little water won't hurt. I'll take whatever they've got between two pieces of bread. And I'll tell you what else." He touched her cheek with the backs of his fingers.

The look in his eyes made her throat go dry. "What else?"

"For taking such good care of me you've got at least a week comin'."

"A week…"

He nodded. "Comin'. Yeah. And don't think I can't do just as good on one leg as I can on two."

"I wouldn't... You don't have to. I mean, this changes—"

"Nothing." He gave her a quick kiss. "I hate crutches. I'll be off them in no time."

She patted his flat, hard stomach. "I'll be back in no time."

"Sure you don't wanna throw me in the shower first?"

"Whatever you need."

"The list is short, but the need..." He kissed her again. "You'd better get going while you can."

"I'll drop you off in the bathroom on my way to the door."

He laughed. "Hell of a date."

Moonlight brightened the parking lot. Skyler had the keys in her hand, and she was going to gather some of his stuff from his pickup. He'd trusted her with his hat and now his pickup. She eyed the sleek topper that covered the pickup bed. The contents of a cowboy's pickup probably revealed a lot about him, she thought. Not that she would ever snoop, but she had to wonder what Trace carried with him on the road. What would it hurt if she took a peek?

Maybe she'd find a few books or magazines, and she'd learn more about his interests. Maybe he kept clippings, and she could learn more about his career. He didn't brag himself up—old-fashioned cowboy modesty was rare these days—but it would be fun to see what he'd done, what sportswriters had said about him. It would have to be fun. He was a fun guy.

Or maybe she'd find pictures of some of the horses he'd trained. Maybe family pictures. Maybe girlfriends. She was just curious, wanted to find out what he liked and who and why. She could ask him, of course. She could be nosy without being downright sneaky.

Or she could act her age, as her mother used to say. She could mind her own business and take him his boots and his duffel bag and just…get hold of herself. Because she had plans. Some of them might work out, some might not, but she had to make her own way and she was beginning to see her way. *Her* way. Trace Wolf Track was a distraction, and maybe the mustang was, too. Lovely distractions—*necessary* distractions from the widow's box she'd built for herself—but they were just passing through, crossing her path.

And Skyler was moving out of the box. She was going to start getting real very soon now, start making it on her own. She really did have a life to live. Not as a princess or a caretaker or a guardian—and certainly not as a snoop.

She'd almost majored in journalism years ago, but even when she'd dropped the academic plan by the wayside, she'd kept up with her photography. She didn't enjoy bookkeeping or ranch management, but she'd taken them on out of necessity, and she could actually see herself setting those roles aside. The ZQ Ranch. With the fall would come the time for selling calves and maybe everything else unless Mike decided to get with the program. Skyler would lay out a program. Do or die, she would say. And then she would call for the gate.

She smiled to herself as she located the boots and the bag exactly where Trace had said they would be. She locked the pickup, gave the topper one last glance and headed back inside.

"Food's here."

Skyler stowed the boots and the duffel bag next to her rolling suitcase in the corner of the room and set the takeout bag near Trace's foot, propped on the edge of the bed. He was sitting in the room's only chair, back to the door. She'd noticed his jeans on the bathroom floor along with a rumpled towel, noticed his powerful shoulders, all buff and bare as she'd walked past him.

"Oh, good," she said, staring at the purpling skin that disappeared beneath layers of taping on his foot. "You're icing."

"It's okay to turn around." She heard the amusement in his voice. "I'm RICE-ing. Rest, ice, compression, elevate."

"You've done this before." She turned, sat on the bed, looked up and smiled.

"Many times." He closed his eyes and dropped his chin to his chest, his arms resting on the wooden arms of the chair. His hair fell over his forehead in dark, wet tendrils. "More than I can count."

She gave herself a moment to take in the sight of him, during which her only thought was, *Man, oh, man.* But what she said was, "Boxer briefs. It's true. We do wonder." They were black. Sexy. She glanced up and found him smiling. Reading her mind. So much for the humble cowboy. "How's the swelling?"

"Alive and well."

"Well, I have something for you."

She patted his "ol' hairy leg" in parting, moved behind him, laid her hands on his shoulders and pressed her fingers into knotted muscles. He groaned, a blend of protest and pleasure. She had done this before, more times than she could count, and she was good at it. She pushed hard with the heels of her hands, dug deep with her thumbs until his muscles gave a little and a little more until finally his shoulder sagged and his head fell back and rested on her stomach with a great sigh. She pressed her thumbs into his nape and tunneled her fingers into his hair, massaging his scalp, drawing heavy thoughts up, up and away. He gave a soft, throaty sound. Pure pleasure.

"Something smells good," he said long moments later. "Besides you."

"Comfort food." She took a foam box from the bag and made a presentation of it with a cloth napkin and tableware—she'd firmly nixed paper and plastic. "Meat loaf and mashed potatoes."

"I'm not real..." He glanced up and quickly changed his tune. "Perfect."

"Nobody is," she said with a smile. "But physically—well, except for the ankle and the knee... Otherwise, I have to say, you're pretty damn close."

"I clean up pretty good, but perfect is a tall order." He stabbed his fork into the potatoes, took a taste and then dug in ravenously. He'd eaten half his food before he came up for air and took notice of her takeout box. "What've you got?"

"Chicken with wild rice. Here. Taste." She reached across the divide and held a forkful to his lips. He approved the sample with a nod. "Trade?" He shook his head, still chewing. "This late, these were the choices."

"It's good. Try this." He gave her meat loaf dipped in potatoes. "Hmm?"

"Mine's better."

He shrugged. "We'll get started early. I don't like to hang around on the last night. On a good night, you collect your winnings and hit the road. Bad nights, you just hit the road." He spared his ankle a glance as he raked his potatoes with his fork. "But I won't be pushing anything with this foot, not for a few days at least. I don't think I tore much. Maybe a little something, not much." He stabbed the meat loaf. "Ten days until Cheyenne. I never miss that one."

"What's special about that one?"

"It's Cheyenne. You ever been?"

"I've been to Cheyenne."

"You live in Wyoming, and you haven't been to the Cheyenne Frontier Days?" He shook his head, frowning, couldn't fathom such an oversight. "I'll take you with me. You'll see what's special. It's one of the granddaddies."

"You owe me two days."

"Starting tomorrow," he reminded her around a bite of meat loaf. "And like I said, I can do better on my end of the deal."

"Tomorrow you'll still be RICE-ing."

"Mmm. You were right. I didn't think about food."

"Because, there's no *F* in RICE, and you're following doctor's orders to the letter."

"How about we add a little therapy that starts with *S? RICES.* End the day on a high note with a little—"

"*Elevate* is high."

"So am I." He leered. "You could take advantage of me so easy."

"No, the *I* is for *ice,*" she said as she closed the lid on her supper. "My home court. I'm the ice queen."

"No problem. I come equipped with an ice pick."

"I have one, too. Mine has my name engraved on it." She stood and moved to the highboy, where she unloaded the box. "I was Winter Carnival Queen. Also Miss Northern Lights, Princess Kay of the Milky Way, Miss Harmon County, Lake Festival Princess, Miss Potato—" she smiled to herself, touched his shoulder on her way back to the bed "—Head."

He gave an appreciative whistle. "That's a lot of… Potato Head?"

"I got a complete makeover out of that one. New nose, eyes, lips, big funny ears." She'd wiped the smile off her face, but it was still in her eyes. "They all came in a box."

"Are you gonna crown me if I laugh?"

"Maybe."

"Talk about perfect, that's you." He set his empty box on the floor beside his chair, and then his gaze claimed hers. "Seriously, you could be queen of the world. Mine, anyway."

Cowboy flattery. Next he'd be calling her Miss Skyler. Or worse, ma'am.

"There's always some kind of scholarship attached," she explained. "That's how I paid for a year of college. I dropped out when I married one of the judges." She gave a perfunctory smile. "I was only first runner-up in that contest. I didn't marry him right away."

"He was married?"

"He was a widower. He hired me as a nanny for the summer." She shook off the memory and scooped his empty box off the floor. "What's the *R* for? *Rest?* Time to rest."

"I don't take too well to nannying."

"That was my nursing voice." She unzipped the side pocket of her bag and took out her toiletry case. "My nanny voice is more like, *I'm going to count to*

*three. One. I know one of your feet hurts. Use the
other one. Two.*"

"I'm *going*." He flicked the ice pack out of the
way and groaned pitifully as he lifted his foot off
the bed.

"You want your toothbrush?"

"You're cold, woman. I might as well be sleepin'
with an ice pack."

"Only twenty minutes at a time."

"That's not what I meant."

"It's what I meant." She took her toothpaste and
night cream out and sat down on the toilet to pull her
boots off. "Nursing voice again."

"Will that be the one bringing me my toothbrush?
Most nurses I know are warm and tender."

"You trust me to rummage around in your personal stuff?"

"I'm *dying* to have you rummage around in my
personal stuff."

She smiled at herself in the mirror. She'd forgotten
how much fun this game could be.

He was in bed when she brought him the water
and toothbrush. He laughed and shook his head and
said this was "damned humiliating," but he complied
with her directions in return for her agreement to stop
fussing around.

He patted the empty side of the bed. "You lie down
beside me."

"Will you be a good boy?"

"No. But I'll be a good man." He pulled the

covers back on what would be her side of the bed and smoothed his hand over the stiff white sheet. "Come here. I'll show you." She hesitated. "Are you afraid of me, Skyler?"

"No," she said, and then she glanced at the ceiling. "A little. Or maybe it's me." She laughed nervously. She'd been a dutiful wife for fifteen years, but she hadn't been pleasured by anyone but herself in... She couldn't remember the last time. "Maybe you should be afraid."

"Maybe I should. I don't know much about royalty."

"Why did I tell you that?" She shook her head.

"Come here. We've only got this one bed, honey, so I guess we'll just have to make the best of it. And, hell, I'm..." He made a sweeping gesture toward the foot of the bed. "So make yourself comfortable. I'm harmless. Do you generally sleep in your jeans?"

"I'll take a shower and, um...I'll show you what I sleep in."

"Mmm. I love surprises."

Her Joe Boxer pajamas were hardly sexy. Long pink-and-blue-striped pants and a jersey tank with an aptly placed pink heart weren't what she would have chosen if she'd planned to spend the night with a man. She wasn't sure what she would have worn. If she'd planned it, she would have shopped Victoria's Secret catalog.

But she wouldn't have planned it. Dreamed it, maybe, but never planned it. Her best-laid plans would not have led her to a bed nearly filled with an injured rodeo cowboy. They would have led her back to the bed she felt safe in, the one that was hers alone. Had been ever since Tony had—over Skyler's objections—banished her to another bedroom.

He'd been a proud man, and it was hard to watch him go down with that particular ship. The SS *Pride*. But Skyler had stood her ground when he'd asked her to hire a nurse. They couldn't afford it, but she hadn't told him that. She'd said she wanted to take care of him herself, which, to her abiding shame, hadn't been completely true. Not every day. There were days when she'd imagine him getting better and others when she'd wish it would all be over.

Damn the memory. Why couldn't she just do what she wanted to do for a change? She'd once been a princess. Where was her crown when she needed it?

She spritzed herself with the scent of cherry blossoms, turned to the mirror and lifted her damp hair away from her face with splayed fingers. The hair dryer had cleared the steam away and she watched her hair fall bit by silky bit. She looked fine. Once she got over herself, she would feel fine, and she would remember what it meant to be a whole woman.

When she returned to the bedroom, his face was turned away and he had kicked the makeshift prop off the end of the bed. He was asleep. She took a seat cushion from a chair and made a wider shelf for his bandaged foot, arranging pillows until they formed the perfect mound. She moved his leg gently and covered him. He hardly moved when she stretched out beside him between crisp sheets chilled by the air-conditioning he'd asked her to jack up. He had all the pillows.

The vapor light from the parking lot streamed through the space between the blackout curtains and cast a white glow across his handsome face. His arm folded behind his head was like an open invitation to tuck in close to his side within a hair's breadth of touching him. His body was a radiator. He smelled tangy, like oranges and clove. Without opening his eyes he lowered his arm, and she lifted her head and found a pillow in the pocket of his shoulder.

Trace woke to a soft gray light, a hard ache and a killer throbbing all wrapped up in a thick analgesic haze. He could either try to sort it all out, or lie still and hope some part of it would go away. He tried the second option first, but something moved, and it wasn't him. He turned his muzzy head and ran into a pile of pale hair the color of the morning sky. He breathed its scent and imagined a tree full of flowers.

She lifted her face as though he'd spoken her name. Her lips parted, and he greeted her with a kiss. She turned herself to him, pressed her whole sweet body tight against his. He gave another kiss and another as he shifted to take her in his arms and keep her from slipping away. She felt real, but he didn't trust anything he was feeling. He'd wished the pain away, but if she was part of the reason for it, he'd take the wish back. *Throb on.*

He buried his fingers in her soft hair to keep them from tearing into her clothes. He knew who she was, but not really. He remembered how they'd come to this moment, but not really. *Leave it at that,* he told himself. *Leave it and take it. Pain comes with pleasure, and this feels like the best of both.*

She had the advantage. She was lying on his arm. While she explored his chest with her upper hand and teased his belly with the back of her lower one, he made his advances with one arm tied behind her back and his other hand tangled in her hair. He was riding without reins. She discovered his nipple and sissified it with a kindly cruel fingernail, dragging an unmanly sound out of him, as if he was down and defenseless and didn't mind at all. He was about to even things up, but she suddenly slipped her hand into his Jockey shorts. For a second, he didn't know where his next breath was coming from.

She hardly moved. He didn't dare move. They were poised on a glittering runway. *Take off or turn around?*

He held her head in his hand and she held his. Thinking was not an option.

His kiss was his invitation. His tongue showed her what he wanted to do with her, what he would give her, what he hoped for in return.

But have it your way, Skyler. Whatever you want, have it now. Have it all.

Her hand closed around his throttle and moved down over him at the end of the runway and drew him up, up, up. His pain gave him pause. A modicum of control. Enough to allow him to withdraw his hand—carefully, carefully, no pain for her—and slide it over her hip, bring those silly pants of hers down, down, down and seek smooth, soft skin and springy hair and parting thighs and a lovely damp place. His thumb brought out the best in her, the wetness that would ease his entrance. But he would take his time, discover her a little at a time, feel the heat inside her and listen to her growing pleasure and make it crest and wash over her. He could do this for her without backing off, without turning around.

It was her turn to sound the need in her, a wordless, throaty plea that drove him to take her hand from him. He wanted her in the worst way but he wasn't prepared. She needed him in the best way, and he would do his best for her and hope for the same in return. She took him inside her before he could think what that was—his best, his hope, the possibility of some return on his investment.

Thinking was not an option.

They were in the air now. She was a high roller and he was a long rider. This was win-win, he thought. His pain intensified his pleasure, but he wanted to keep that to himself. He could not know whether there was pain for the woman who took him inside her, but

if there was, he wanted to ease it. He wanted her to
feel him fully and know him tenderly. He meant to
give all pleasure, no pain. And no consequences.

He truly meant to.

Chapter Five

They lay side by side. He hadn't said a word, but she could hear his mind galloping over a washboard. Up, down, up, down. She felt the words in his heartbeat. *What now, what now, what now.* No narcotic fog killed his good conscience. He was that kind of man.

She was almost sure of it.

It was about the only thing she was sure of right now, except that she felt wonderful, and she didn't want any part of that feeling taken away. *Give me this euphoric feeling for five more minutes. I deserve that much.*

She laid her hand on his beautiful chest—a little soft hair, a lot of hard muscle—and felt his heart beating against her palm. She lifted her head and kissed the near side of his chest. Then she rested her chin on the kiss and blew softly on his nipple until it behaved the same way its brother had.

He groaned.

"How's your ankle?" she whispered.

"What ankle?"

She kissed him again, same spot, near the bump she had silently whistled to attention.

"Once more, and I'm all over you," he said. "Third time's the charm."

"The other one didn't need three." She glanced up smiling. "But they're both charming."

His eyes were closed. He lay still and quiet for what started out as an easy moment, but it stretched and stretched until it began to smack of misgiving, the sour-tasting answer to *What now?*

Keep it to yourself, then, she thought. The morning had begun with a kiss and that was hers to keep. As for intercourse, she'd made the call. If there was one thing she did not want to hear it was an apology.

"I'll do better next time," he said at last.

"Better?"

"Much better." He tucked his free arm beneath his head and looked her in the eye. "All over you."

"I'm going to hold you to that."

"Me, too." He frowned slightly. "Do you have anything against condoms?"

"I don't know."

"You're kidding."

She shook her head. "It's never been an issue for me."

"Damn." He drew a deep breath. "It's…kind of an issue for everybody, don't you think?"

She nodded. "But I'm just getting back in the game."

His eyes were too keen, too perceptive. She wished she could say something sharp and sassy, but he'd just turned her fear of being diminished somehow on its head, and nothing she could say would hide that from him. She felt good. No regrets, no remorse, no guilt. She'd wanted him, and that was that.

Better next time.

She turned her cheek to his chest, closed her eyes and wondered how much better it could be.

Another time—maybe next time—she could say such a thing, but not now. She wanted to keep *now* just as it was. The end of a long, lonely drought.

The promise of more rain.

The pickup lurched as the ball hitch coupled with the horse trailer. Trace was ready to disembark. "Relax," Skyler ordered. "I've got this."

"You sure?" He settled back into his seat. "The doors can be tricky. Call me if you need me, and I'll hop right out." She gave him a parting thumbs-up, and he added, "His name is Jack."

"Jack loads like a dream," she reported as she buckled herself behind the wheel.

"Figured he would. He likes you." He slid his seat

back as soon as she started the pickup. "His registered name is Ball in the Jack. When I first heard that, I thought, what were they thinking? Then I saw it written out on paper. Not exactly what I pictured." He chuckled. "Still doesn't make much sense."

She smiled. "It's an old dance."

"You know how to do it?"

"Really old dance, like early 1900s. I don't go back quite that far, but I do know how to do it. I took dance lessons growing up." She signaled in advance of the on-ramp. "There's a song, too."

"Really? How does it go?"

"I've forgotten."

"No, you haven't. Come on. A few bars." He reached across the center console and tapped her arm. "How 'bout if I take you to a few bars? You'd be singin' after how many stops? Two? Three?" When he couldn't get more than a tight smile out of her, he drew back and settled in for the long haul. "What is it, a game? Something girls play, I'll bet. Totally innocent. Ball in the jack."

"It was a railroad term." She hadn't intended to pull out the trivia file, but with a hundred empty miles ahead, might as well fill them from what Tony liked to call her store of apropos-of-nothing facts. "It was a signal to go faster, and it wasn't ball *in*. It was *ballin' the jack,* spelled just the way you thought. The jack was the locomotive—the jackass that pulled the load—and the highball signal meant *go fast*. So the dance…" She lifted one shoulder. "It's actually kind of cute."

"When do I get to see it?"

"Let's see." She glanced left and right. Herefords grazed on one side and a rocky red bluff flanked the other. "Where's a Redbox when you need one? *For Me and My Gal*. Gene Kelly and Judy Garland. Early 1940s, I think. I'll have to check the date."

"I believe you. I'm partial to old Westerns, but I couldn't quote you any dates. Maybe a line or two. 'If God didn't want them sheared, he wouldn't have made them sheep.'" He grinned at her, gave her about three seconds and then whistled a dozen notes from "The Theme from the Magnificent Seven."

He was a good whistler.

"So you like trains?"

"My husband was interested in trains. I have lots of books about trains." She thought for a moment. "Go fast. Go all out," she mused. "It's a good name for a horse."

"If he doesn't mind the jackass part." He shifted his legs and pushed a seat button, but it wasn't getting him anywhere. He was as far back as he was going to get. "Speed isn't Jack's strong suit. He's quick and he's agile. Put some cow sense on him, and he's a cuttin' horse. He'll double my investment."

"Do you have cattle?"

"I keep a few head around for working horses."

"Around where?" She shook her head. "I don't even know where you live."

"You wrote the check."

"And handed it to Michael. Along with a few words about the amount and what it was for. Not the who or the where. Just the what. So tell me where."

"A few miles outside of Newcastle."

"I love that Black Hills country. Do you…"

"Yep." Lips pressed firmly he nodded slowly. "I live alone."

"Good to know."

"I'll bet." He turned to her, eyes smiling. "You carnival queens are all alike. Kiss the clown first, ask questions later."

"Touché."

"Just kidding. Some things you just know about a person. You don't have to take an application." He slapped the console for emphasis. "Right? Like if he's a cowboy, he's always goin' down the road. Big ego, little brain."

"Not always. They have their modest moments." She slid him a smile. "If she's a stepmother, she's mean and ugly."

"Not always. Not after she washes up and gets her face on." He tapped her arm with a loose fist. "Wait till you meet my new stepmother. Did I tell you she's a soldier? Logan did real good this time."

For a moment he was quiet. He took his hat off and tossed it onto the backseat, shifted his long legs. He was uncomfortable. She was pushing the speed limit, but she wished she could go all out, *ballin' the jack,* fly low and get him down the road.

"I've never met a dairy princess," he said. "Is that how you learned your way around an ice-cream cone?"

"Frozen custard." She flashed him a smile. "If she's a dairy princess, she must be a butterball."

"I met a pork queen once. We were both riding in a parade. Fourth of July. She was a firecracker. Bright, wild, funny as hell."

"Sounds like a corker."

"And she was no porker." He wanted a laugh for that, and she obliged. "She was looking for scholarship money, too. She's probably a bank president or a rocket scientist by now."

"Or the mother of a couple of kids and the wife of a—"

"—rich pig farmer." He chuckled. "A lot of people look at life as a ladder, and that's kind of the way I've tried to go. More up the road than down. But lately..." He leaned back and rested his head. "Logan says it's a circle. I tell him I'm not interested in chasing my tail or following behind anybody else's. He says it's not like that. Doesn't have to be, anyway." He made a high-level gesture. "So here I am, standing on the top of Hill Number Thirty, and I'm thinkin', he's right. There's always a lineup for the ladder and then somebody on every rung. You make a circle, you're not lookin' at a bunch of tails." He rolled his head in her direction. "Is this what happens when you get a little age on you? Ego switches places with brain?"

"You're asking *me?*"

"I'm not asking unless that's what it takes. You want me to ask?"

"I don't see what difference it makes."

He chuckled. "Neither do I, but you've been chokin' on it, honey, so spit it out."

"I'll be forty," she chirped and gave a *dare you* look. "In three years."

"Damn, you're well preserved." He winked at her, and her stony stare melted away. "I figure I'm at least that in cowboy years. You start countin' the miles I've put on this carcass and all the repair work they've had to do on it, hell, I'm old enough to be your…" He smiled. "Whatever you need right now."

"You're right. It feels good to get it out. That and the beauty-queen thing. I don't know why." She glanced at his knees. "Is it bothering you much?"

"It never bothered me at all."

"Your *ankle*."

"Oh, yeah, that bothers me. It would feel good to get it up."

"I could help you with that."

"I know. Let's pull over."

"Do you want to stop now, or wait till we get to the ranch? We're fifteen miles out."

"It's throbbing pretty good."

"Your call," she said.

"I've waited my whole life to hear those words. I'm gonna call backseat. I can't wait fifteen miles."

She pulled off the road and helped him get situated on the narrow club cab seat with his taped foot braced against the side window.

"You should have been back here all along," she told him as she tucked his duffel bag behind his shoulders.

"We wouldn't've talked. I wouldn't've known what *ballin' the jack* means or how old you are. How old did you say you were when the song first came out?" She swatted his shoulder. "Watch it, woman. My hours on the injured list number in the single digits. And then I'm comin' for you."

"Thanks for the warning," she said as she climbed behind the wheel. "That's an eight seconds I won't want to miss."

"You know what, Skyler?" he called out from the backseat. "You're not just another pretty face."

"Nice little place you've got here." Trace grabbed the front seat and the back door and gingerly levered himself to the ground. She'd parked the pickup and horse trailer next to a corral with a loafing shed, which were only the beginning of a series of pens and outbuildings. He reached into the passenger seat for his hat, put it on and surveyed the rest of the setup while he adjusted the brim against the afternoon sun. The two-story rock and milled-log house was big enough for a good-size family, but it was the smaller house partnered with its own rickety barn that caught Trace's eye.

"Who lives in the other house? Ranch fore-man?"

"The foreman would be me. I'm everything but the owner and the hired help."

"You don't own it, and you work for free?"

"I don't own the ranch, but the main house has my name on it. Mine and the bank's," she announced with a sweeping gesture. She nodded toward the smaller one. "That's the original house, the home place. That's Mike's, along with the land and the livestock."

"You aren't partners in the ranching business? That's what he said when he handed me that check. 'My partner handles the finances.'"

"It's complicated." She motioned for him to follow her.

He stood his ground. He wasn't one to tag along on the heels of a shutdown.

She reversed her direction along with her tone. "I don't know how else to explain it," she said as she pulled his arm over her shoulder and slipped hers around his waist. "Come on, just a few steps. He's right around the corner."

"It's none of my business."

"I mean the horse."

He could've limped along by himself, but what fun would that be? He wasn't leaning on her. Now that she was coaxing rather than bossing, he was enjoying her attention.

"Trace Wolf Track, meet Wild Thing."

The sorrel-faced "flea-bitten" gray stood on the shady side of the loafing shed. He wanted shade, but there was no way he was going inside that three-sided trap all by his lonesome. He was more than the sum of his handsome parts—sleek and sturdy, regal head, beautifully appointed with black mane, tail and legs, and the generous application of red specks to a gray coat that tagged him "flea-bitten."

Trace grimaced. "Wild Thing?"

Skyler only had eyes for the horse.

"I read about the competition, and I thought I'd go over there and take some pictures, maybe work up a photo essay or even a video. From the first moment I saw him, I thought we had some kind of connection. I felt like I was supposed to take him home, like we could learn something from each other. There were a couple of other people there picking out horses for the competition, but he wanted nothing to do with them. He seemed to choose me."

The leap from *hard to explain* to *easy to believe* sent gravity packing, changing Skyler's whole demeanor. Trace smiled. "Don't tell me he made your heart sing."

"How did you know?" Without taking her eyes from the horse, she smiled wistfully. "I felt like Snow White, beloved of wild creatures. We got along really well at first, that initial waltz in the forest, and then we hit the castle wall."

"What happened, princess? You whistled and he wouldn't come?"

She tipped her head and squinted against the sun. "You like the way I set that up for you?"

"Beautiful." A breeze toyed with her blush-colored hair, and she lifted her hand to catch it or salute him or shade one eye. She might have been trying to wink at him and couldn't remember how it was done. God, he wanted to kiss her. "Are you afraid of each other?"

She lifted one shoulder. "I'm very comfortable on a horse. You saw that yourself."

"Yeah, but this guy really is a wild thing. Maybe he does connect with you on a gut level, but he doesn't choose to carry you on his back. Far as he knows, anything that jumps on his back is out to kill him."

"I've been all about showing him that I come in peace. I've managed to halter him. That's huge."

"It is. Then what?"

"I tried to longe him, but I think it was too soon. Either that or I did something that scared him off. I don't know what. I've taken it slow and easy, and he's even taken food from my hand."

"So he's like a pet."

"Absolutely not. Once I have him under saddle, I'm not going to ask him to be anything but a horse. I don't want to break his spirit. I like a horse with spirit."

"Are you out to win this thing? You could've adopted a mustang. You didn't have to sign on for the training contest."

"It isn't just a contest. It's a cause. And it's a

personal challenge. Horses have always been an important part of my life—maybe the best part—but starting a horse from square one is something I've never done. I went to the Double D thinking I would take some pictures and talk to some people, and I found a story I wanted to be part of. I've had some ups and downs, but that's all part of the story."

"You don't care about winning?"

She folded her arms over the corral rail, rested her chin on her sleeve and considered the mustang. "I wouldn't *mind* winning. If that helps any."

"Does that help you any, big guy?" Trace called out to the horse. "Don't worry about being all you can be. Good enough is good enough."

"I stopped taking contests too seriously a long time ago," Skyler said. "Trophies collect dust. It's all about how you play the game. I really believe that."

"I like to play hungry." He scanned the empty corrals. "What else have you got here? Since we're just past square one, any chance of a round pen?"

She grinned. "There's an *almost* square one. It's pretty small."

"Show me."

"Why don't we turn Jack out with my wild child here? Wouldn't that give us—"

Trace laughed. "You really don't have a name for him, do you?"

"It hasn't come to me."

"Guess he must be holding back on you, huh? Connection interrupted." He turned and leaned back against the corral. "Now, my dad would want him to have a good name. But Logan's an Indian, and I'm just a cowboy. I don't think that horse cares what you call him as much as *how* you call him. Wild or tame, he's not your baby." He shook his head, grinning. "I gotta say *thing* and *child* don't work for me, but the horse doesn't care what word you use."

She turned away from him and said quietly, "I want a copy of your father's book. Can I buy it online?"

"I'll hook you up with a copy."

"No, I'll order it."

"Suit yourself. I buy them by the case. Don't tell Logan that. I've given a bunch of them away."

"It's too bad your father isn't aware of the compliment you're paying him. You're a good man."

"I'm doing it for the horses." He leaned his shoulder against the corral and faced her. "Okay, for Logan because he put a lot of work into it, but he speaks for the horse. Maybe that sounds hokey, but it's true."

"I can't wait to read it," she said quickly, suddenly a little girl, eager to please. "What do you think? Put Jack in with…" She turned to the horse. "I don't have the heart to name him when I have to give him up at the end of the competition. I'm just a foster mother."

Trace laughed. "He doesn't need a mother, and if he did, he wouldn't *choose* you."

She waved his words away. "Forget I said that choosing part."

"And he'd take Jack's company over yours any

day, which is why we're not putting them together. Not yet."

She couldn't let go. "I guess it sounded silly when I said he chose me. Or *hokey*. Some people would think that, but I know we had a moment. It was like he recognized me. *Hey, Skyler, I'm over here.*"

"A dog will choose you over his own kind, but not a horse." He wanted off this ride. Considering what he was feeling for her and what she wanted from him, the whole mystical connection was a tight fit at the moment. He wanted to take it off and start over.

He reached for her hand. "Did we decide that I was gonna lay over for a while? Because I'd like to lay my head down and put my foot up."

"I'm sorry." She slipped her arm around his waist. "Here I stand yakking and I should be taking care of my guest."

"Just point me to a piece of floor and maybe a chair, and I'll take care of the rest."

Trace allowed the woman to hold the back door open for him since he'd surrendered the use of his arms to the damn crutches. He promised himself he'd be off them tomorrow. He'd get his legs under him, get his head on straight, help Skyler and the mustang negotiate their wall, enjoy their company for a day or two and then head on down the road. He'd keep in touch, sure. She was one hell of a woman, but a couple of days and he was already in pretty deep. He knew how to rehab an ankle, but his heart was the last part of himself he'd lay on the line. He wasn't ready.

Mike walked into the kitchen eating a sandwich. The look in his eyes said he'd been expecting playmates and here came the cat. But he recovered quickly.

"Hey, Skyler, looks like you brought one of them hard-luck cowboys home with you. Need any help?"

"No, thanks." Trace claimed the closest kitchen chair. "Speak for yourself, kid. A hard-luck cowboy isn't the guy who takes first in his event."

"Way to go." Mike took a glass down from a cupboard. "Must've been the buckle-bunny stampede afterward that took you down."

"It was a bad landing. Second one in less than a week."

"Plus your birthday. Maybe the gods are trying to tell you something, Trace."

"As long as I keep winning, we're good. That's a message I can take to the bank."

"How's the hay coming, Mike?" Skyler asked, and then she turned to Trace. "Can I get you something?" He shook his head, bemused. *Two men, two questions, one breath.*

"Grady wanted to finish knocking that grass down on the west side," Mike reported as he pulled a jug of milk from the refrigerator. "I figured I'd ride along the creek up to the north fence line and take a head count, but the morning got away from me, and now it's too hot."

"Grady's still out there cutting hay," Skyler pointed out.

"In an air-conditioned cab. 'Course, he's an old man. He deserves all the amenities."

"Grady doesn't use the AC in the tractor. He says it's a waste of gas."

"So, Trace." Mike glanced past the glass he was filling. "What do you think of Skyler's latest project? She had it going on pretty good, and then she kinda got frustrated. Thought she might throw in the towel." He slapped the plastic cap on the jug with a flat hand. "Since horse trainers don't figure into the budget."

"I like him," Trace said. "We'll see if I can help get things going again."

Mike took a drink. "How long are you staying?"

Skyler snatched the abandoned milk jug off the counter and spared her stepson a cutting glance on her way to the refrigerator. "How long have you been rude?"

"I didn't mean…" Mike flashed an empty palm. "Hell, Trace, you're welcome to stay as long as you want. Especially with…" He turned surrender into sympathy with a gesture toward Trace's ankle. "You gotta stay off your feet. You need some ice or something?"

"I'm good, thanks. I just need to get down and get the foot up. Let the air out of the balloon."

"Let's find you a pillow and a prop," Skyler said

as she stowed the milk. She patted Mike's arm. "How long can *you* stay?"

"I can stay for supper, but I'm going out after that."

Mike's delivery struck Trace as a little too straight for a joke, which meant they would be three for supper. Disappointed, he followed Skyler into the living room and dropped his crutches beside a big leather chair with an ottoman.

"Right here is fine."

She spun on her heel. "I can do better than this."

"I'm sure you can, but I don't want to put anyone out." He sat down and swung his feet up to the cushy footrest. "Ahh, elevation."

"This is my house. I get to say who's welcome to stay and for how long." She knelt beside him and eased the loosely laced boot off his bum foot. He started to tell her he could do it, but the words wouldn't come. "I hope you'll stay as long as you can, and I don't want you to worry about the horse."

"Do I look worried?"

"No, but I have a feeling worry doesn't show on you."

"It shows on you." She gave him a curious look— part pouty, part puzzled—and he smiled. "It doesn't look bad. It just looks like something you don't need. Something a man wants to take away from you." He laid his head back and closed his eyes. "You should catch yourself in the mirror when you're having fun. Makes my heart sing."

"I'd groan, but I don't want to seem ungracious."

"That, and you started it."

Skyler returned to the kitchen and to Mike, who had finished his first sandwich and was building a second.

"I thought you liked Trace," she said quietly.

"I do. But don't you think he's a little young for you?"

"I don't think I need to think about it. I just met him."

"I just don't want you to get hurt by some..." Skyler shot him a *shut up* look, and he lowered his voice. "I know we're not doin' too well financially, and I don't want some guy to come along and add insult to injury."

"I don't know what to say. I don't even see a connection," she said absently, her mind switching to meal planning. But she stopped, backtracked. "Didn't you just break up with a woman who was a few years older than you?"

"She broke up with me."

She offered a token nod. "If I'd felt a need to make a case, I could rest it right there."

"Whatever that means."

"I was giving you the benefit of the doubt, but it really doesn't matter. We don't have to protect each other. We're grown-ups."

"You're not the type to have a fling, Skyler, but you're easy pickin's right now," he said quietly.

"*Eas*—"

"I don't mean—"

"Keep your voice down." She lowered hers to his level. "We're not having this conversation. It isn't happening. You're going to ride fence, and I'm going to try to figure out how we can keep Grady on through the summer. And my guest is off-limits to you until you cut the crap." She nodded toward the sandwich on its way to his mouth. "So I hope your refrigerator has something in it besides beer."

"I'm just sayin'."

Have it. The last word is yours.

But her pointed glance at the back door was the last say.

And Trace—who hadn't heard everything, but he'd heard enough—bottled up the last laugh.

Chapter Six

"Keep him moving, Skyler. Keep talking to him. We want him to go easy, and he's not there yet." Trace let the camera run in video mode while he tested buttons. "How do you make this thing pull out? From close in to—" *Zoop, zip.* "Never mind. I got it."

Skyler was patient, and he had all the time in the world for watching the two of them play off each other. If this was her way of stepping away from her worries, it had to be working for her because she wasn't trying to rush the groundwork the way most people did. He'd told her to forget about the latest traveling trainer and his expensive two-day clinic or two-hour private consultation and horse tune-up. Throw away the video that promised a five-day miracle. There was no substitute for time and patience, and Skyler seemed willing to commit to both. He liked that about her.

Along with just about everything else. He wouldn't mind hanging around for a couple of days—time to help her out and let her come to terms with what she liked about him—but Trace could easily run out of time and patience if Mike wanted to be a pain in the ass. Trace's place was about two hours' drive, which put Skyler in his territory. This was Wyoming. Not too many places had fewer women per square mile.

He sat on the roof of his pickup using his bent knee as a tripod. She'd set the camera for the soft sunlight of late afternoon, and he'd set her up with a coil of double-braided marine rope and a few instructions.

"He's going easy now, Trace. I can feel it. You're groovin', aren't you, big boy?"

He smiled behind the camera, partly for the pleasure of seeing the beautiful dappled horse canter in a circle with Skyler at the center. They were both "going easy." She swung the end of the rope to keep him moving. He was unfettered, and she was undaunted. But his smile was mostly for the way she said his name, the way her voice shined it up somehow. *Going easy* described the feel of moving through the day as though they'd been together through many days and nights.

"Groovin'?" Trace chuckled. "Sounds like I found myself a hippie."

"Child of a hippie." She flipped a few feet of rope through the air and made it dance behind the horse to keep him moving. "That's good," she told him quietly, and then lifted her voice to Trace. "There's hippie blood on my father's side."

"I can tell. Better yet, the horse can tell. You've got that peaceful, easy feelin'."

"Yes, well, my father didn't believe in *bending another to your will*. Isn't that what I'm doing now?"

"If we open the gate, the horse *will* take off."

"So would Jack. A horse is a horse."

"That's right. We bend the will a little so we don't have to break the spirit. Now, drop your arms, turn your shoulder to him, walk away slowly and let's draw him to you."

She executed the draw perfectly, and the horse lowered his head and followed her lead.

"Sweeet," Trace crooned behind the camera.

"Do you think he'd take a treat?"

"What've you got?"

"Nothing." She took a serpentine turn around the pen, and the horse continued to follow. "I just wondered. He should get a reward for this."

"He's not a kid, and he's not a pet, so don't kid yourself. The best treat you can give him is that grass out there."

"And the company of another horse or two. Preferably a herd."

"We'll bring that in later. Right now, you're all he's got. He wants a leader." She stopped, and the horse lowered his muzzle to the ground and sniffed the dirt. "See there? The lead mare chooses the grass. She picks her spot, and everybody else gathers around. Maybe he smells your hippie blood. Take him away from this place and lead him to pastures of plenty."

"I can't keep him in?"

"You have a son who has a well-trained horse. They can get him back in."

She opened the gate to the adjacent small pasture and kept the lead until she had grass underfoot. The horse dashed well past her and celebrated his release by kicking up his heels. Trace kept the camera running, half expecting Skyler—coming to him all bright-eyed and beaming—to do her own little happy dance. He slid down the pickup windshield and met her at the edge of the hood, where he sat, legs dangling.

She put her hands on his thighs and stepped in close. "How're you doing?"

"I'm going easy." He handed her the camera. "I'd take a treat from you."

"What kind would you like?" She smiled up at him. She'd done well and she felt good. "I'm a pretty fair cook."

"I'm easy that way, too. I'm a lousy cook, so anything good is a treat. But I'm guessin' we won't be dining alone."

"We will if I say we will. I decide who grazes where."

"I should be checking in at home." He slid to the ground and claimed the crutches he'd left leaning against the pickup door. "My neighbor watches the place when I'm gone, but I don't like to take advantage."

"Food first." She watched him get himself lined up with the sticks, as though she'd taught him the way he'd taught her. "You said you'd take a treat from me, and I'm going to cook one up. I hope you're hungry."

"Always hungry." But he wasn't going first. The part of him that enjoyed having her hover over him needed to get over it. She was going free and joyful one minute and supervising every move the next, and he really liked her free and joyful. He was on his feet now. He wanted her walking beside him. No leading, no herding. Two people, side by side.

Soon he sat across the kitchen counter from her and took his turn following directions. He sliced an onion, shredded cooked chicken and grated cheese while she put the raw materials to use in the pans on her cooktop. She had a white sauce in the works. She shook a spice bottle over it and cried, "Oh!" She tapped his chopping arm with the bottle. "Watch this."

And he did. Another shake landed red powder in white liquid. The red flecks scattered quickly.

"What does that look like?"

He smiled. Two imaginations, one image. "Your flea-bitten mustang. Is that hot stuff?"

"It's cayenne. A little goes a long way." Her eyes widened. "Cayenne!"

He repeated the word. "Rolls off the tongue pretty good."

"Cayenne. Hot and spicy."

"Just the way I like it." He nodded thoughtfully. "It fits him all the way around, but I'd try it out for a day or two, see how it feels."

"Good idea." She moved the sauce off the burner. "You like salad?"

"I like everything."

Except the way she worried about whether he would like everything. Anybody who knew him would tell her he was low maintenance. When he sat down to the table, he was open to almost anything. She'd been taking meals with somebody who was less so, and he didn't want her confusing him with that somebody. Or any other body, and maybe that in itself was a big want for a guy who wanted for very little. But there it was. He wanted his voice to sound as special to her as hers did to him.

Which was a pretty unsettling thought. A little scary, in fact.

"Oh my gosh."

He looked up as he took his second bite of enchilada and he questioned her *gosh* with a look.

"Too much cayenne."

He lifted one shoulder as he chewed. "Just a little hair of the pony that, uh…" Warm. Hot. *Fire.* He grabbed his glass of water and chugged. "Creeps up on you," he admitted on the tail of a gasp.

"I'm sorry. I got carried away with the whole…

peppery…picture." She reached for his plate. "Let me get you something else."

"No, this is great." He waved her off with his fork en route to his greens. "Especially with this, uh…"

"Salad."

"Salad, yeah. It's got a little fruit in it. Nice touch." He took another bite of enchilada. "Mmm. Could you pass the bread?" He made a stab toward the enchilada with his fork. "Looks real plain and quiet, but it's got a kick to it. Kinda like that dun horse."

"You mean Vegas?"

"Vegas. It's like they say, surprise is the spice of life."

"Variety."

"That, too. See, I wouldn't have tried a green salad that had oranges in it."

"Unless your mouth was burning up. It isn't supposed to be quite this hot." She apologized with a sympathetic look. "I gave it that one extra shake when I noticed how pretty it looked."

"You're an artist." He braved another mouthful of enchilada. The flame had burned down to a nice hot coal. The fact that he could smile was a good sign. "You're also a good cook, Doris."

"Doris?"

"Something my dad used to say. My brother, Ethan, he's a hell of a cook. Which was funny because he is kind of a hell-raiser, big strapping guy. I'm older, but he's taller, built to take on the world." The image of his little brother turned his smile wistful.

His charge, his personal safekeeping until Logan had come along. The woman in their lives had not been the withstanding kind. He stabbed at his salad. "There's no Doris. That's just Logan. He missed the twentieth century." He shrugged. "Maybe it was just because we were three guys bachin' it. You know, if you're good in the kitchen, you're Doris."

"I usually do better than this. Please let me—"

He put his hand up as a stop sign. "Don't try to get between a man and his food." Then he raised his brow. "You know what would be great for dessert?"

"Ice cream?"

"Yeah." He winked at her. "Unless there's a frozen-custard stand in town. How far is it from here?"

"Twenty-three miles to Gillette," she said offhandedly. "Where's your brother?"

"South Dakota. He works with horses, too." He started to elaborate, but, no… "He's getting paid for it now, too."

"That's my dream. Getting paid to do what I love."

"Which is not cattle ranching."

"You noticed," she said quietly, as though she was confessing. "Not the way we've been doing it here. Mmm." She'd thought of something to replace the something she didn't want to think about. "Let's download the video from today. Would you like to see what I took at the wild-horse sanctuary? I've edited it, so it's pretty good. It's not very long. Or maybe

just a few pictures. I'm putting a portfolio together."
She leaned in, smiling. *"Horses."*

"And horse sense." His knowing smile matched
hers.

"I've only just started with your kind of horse
sense," she said. "Rodeo scenes and tight-fitting
jeans."

"I don't wear tight jeans."

"I took a lot of pictures of a lot of jeans, and I have
to say, you wear yours well."

"Guess I'd better stay off the ice cream. Now that
I'm standing on the top of that first hill, I see how
the ass-scape starts spreadin' out." He pointed his
fork at her. "Not yours. You're kind of a tight-ass."

She scowled. "How can you say that?"

"Call 'em like I see 'em, and I like what I see.
Especially the part where you let your guard down
just for me."

"You're sure of that?" She couldn't keep the cor-
ners of her mouth still.

"I'm sure. And I want to know you more. Everything about you."

But he had no smile for her now, and he'd just
killed hers. Completely unintended. He'd meant to
blow her away with his easy cowboy charm, but he'd
missed breezy by a mile. He laid his fork down,
glanced at the clock high on the wall behind her and
shook his head.

"I just tipped my hand. I've never played this hungry, and I'm not real comfortable with it."

"If there's a game going on, I need to know what the rules are," she told him quietly.

"I've already broken the rules." He looked her in the eye. "I'm a stand-up guy. I generally don't let my wants get ahead of my wits."

"Well, your wits were under the weather."

"No. I wanted to be with you in every possible way, and my wits were right there with my wants." He pushed his plate aside. "It won't happen again. Not like that. You said it wasn't an issue with you. What does that mean exactly?"

"There's nothing to worry about, Trace. Really." She reached across the table, laid her hand within his reach. "I wanted to be with you, too. You're right. I'm basically a tight-ass, but being with you…" Her fingers stirred, betraying her uneasiness, telling him she was not easy, not free for the taking. She cleared her throat. "That was my first time in a very long time. And before you, there was never anyone but my husband, who had been sick for a long time."

"Oh, jeez." He stared at her hand, but he wasn't sure he should touch it with his big… "You were like a virgin."

She laughed. "Okay, now you've gone over the edge. I like the cowboy chivalry, but that's pushing it." She drew her hand back and shifted into high gear. "We're just being honest with each other. You want to know all about me, that's another bit of information. Facts are facts. You tell me you've been with X number of women, it's…probably more like an estimate, which isn't exactly a fact, but it's more like—"

"I'm not with anyone now, and that's a fact. Never been married, and that's a fact. Don't have sex without a condom, and that's a fact. Or *was*. I screwed up on that score, but apologizing seems kinda lame."

"You're a good man," she said softly, "and that's a fact."

"You hardly know me."

"Sometimes facts get in the way of the truth. Let X remain a variable. I know what I know. And you're the first man I've ever said this to." She pushed her chair back and pinned him to his with a paralyzing green-eyed stare. "I really want to show you my pictures."

He wanted to laugh, but she was half-serious, and it was the serious half that was demanding its due. "I'll look at anything you want me to see."

Neither of them had finished eating, but he'd done better than she had. He figured it might be a while before he could taste anything again. He followed her lead, taking his plate with him. "I'll help you clean up. What do you use? Machine or man power?"

"I'll take care of it later." She took his plate and clattered them both into the sink. "Would you like a drink? A shot of caffeine or alcohol to get you through my picture show?"

"You wanna rephrase that so I can say yes?"

She laughed. "All of the above it is."

She called the room her office, but Trace didn't see

much of her in it except a few pictures. Everything else was dark green and dull brown. The desk had taken refuge in an alcove bounded by shelves on two sides and a big window in the middle. He pictured Skyler sitting down to the computer, turning her back on a stuffed ram's head and a pair of rainbow trout, mounted separately but hung face-to-face. There was a heavy-duty leather love seat and another chair, more bookshelves, thick carpeting the color of Wyoming mud. This had once been a man's room, and Skyler had kept it that way.

She put a pillow on a footstool, and before she could do the rest for him—she was going there, and he enjoyed the view when she bent down and her top opened up for him—he showed her he could lift his leg just fine. His boot hovered above the pillow.

"I can take it or leave it, honey. The pillow, I mean. The boot's a keeper for now."

"Wouldn't you feel better without…"

"I'd feel better without a lot of things, including the swelling that's gonna happen when I take off that boot."

She went to the bookcase and opened a drop-down shelf. Trace was a whiskey drinker, but since his choice wasn't offered, he sipped the brandy she'd poured and handed to him as though it was some big deal. Okay, so the stuff was pretty smooth. But it didn't suit him.

Skyler's portfolios were a different story. There were horses, sure, and she showed him some shots she'd been hired to take for breeders and show people—beautifully groomed and all squared up with their ears standing at attention. The horses, not the horse people, who were a different breed of animal altogether. She seemed particularly proud of the kid pictures. If there was a kid on the place, she took the kid with a horse as a bonus.

"Look at this one." She slid the book from her knees to his and pointed to a little girl in big glasses, hair in pigtails, decked out in jeans and pink cowboy boots. The mare was twenty years old if she was a day and the string of trophy ribbons hanging from her halter was mostly pink and green. Not a blue one in the bunch. "Her name is Edie. She doesn't see well, but, boy, can she ride. She told me in confidence that the picture wasn't for her. It was a surprise for her grandmother, who loved pictures and had really good eyesight for an elderly person." She grinned. "That's what she said. *Elderly person.* She's six."

"Cute kid." He nodded. "Great picture."

She studied him briefly, as though she was looking for some kind of implication in one comment or the other. Maybe *great* didn't quite cut it.

She closed the book and put it aside. "This isn't what I want to do with my photography, but so far it pays more than the journalism."

"You can do both, can't you?"

"I am. I'm getting more calls from breeders and stud owners for portraits. But every story I sell is one more publishing credit for my résumé. I haven't made a professional-grade video yet, but I will."

"Go on YouTube. I'm on YouTube." He leaned back and sipped his brandy. "So they tell me."

"You haven't looked?"

"I'm not hooked up. I tried it through the phone, but it seemed like more trouble than it was worth." He touched her shoulder just for the feel of her sleeve. She'd showered, put on a silky orange shirt, and she smelled like a flower. "I guess I'm on the thing a few times, but the one people watch the most wasn't my finest hour."

"A bad spill?"

"Spill." He smiled. "That's when you get a little beer on your shirt."

"You don't get kicked around that often, do you? I mean, you're doing very well." She shrugged, cute little apology in her eyes. "I checked online."

"Damn. Yeah, I've won some serious money this year. I'da bragged myself up, but you didn't seem that interested in the standings."

"It's like having your calf-sale check posted. They should just publish the scores."

"Nope. Rodeo isn't like other professional sports. You've gotta earn your pay ride by ride." He drained his glass. "I don't mind. I competed in roping and rough stock for a few years. Decided I wasn't gonna win the all-around, so I decided to go full-bore on my best event. I'm lookin' to take the bareback buckle this year."

"And you're looking good," she said cheerfully as she stood up and took the glass from his hand. "But I won't be looking you up on YouTube. I don't like spills. They can be messy."

"Yeah, but that's part of the draw."

"It can be hard on the horse, too."

"Nobody loves horses more than cowboys." Hearing the words made him laugh. "Correction. *Everybody* loves horses more than cowboys. A champion cowboy rides the most horses. A champion horse bucks off the most cowboys. Put the two together, it's win-win. And I'll tell you what." He raised an instructive finger. "Nobody wants to see that horse get hurt. The cowboy? Nothing like a train wreck to get the crowd's attention." He grinned. "So let's be ballin' the jack, boys."

She glanced at his propped-up foot. "Are you going to sleep in those?"

He nodded. "Gonna die in 'em, too." She turned away laughing. "Where are you going? Hell, I'll take 'em off if—"

"You stay elevated. I'm going to get you another treat."

He laid his head back and closed his eyes. Had to admit, the sofa was more comfortable than anything he had at his place. Maybe he'd buy a new one with some of those winnings she'd found attached to his name. Leather on the furniture was classy. Stuffed animals? Logan had taught him to hunt only for food and to use up every part of anything he killed. He didn't know whether people hunted bighorn sheep for meat. Maybe some lucky cat had chowed down on that pair of kissing trout. Bottom line, he didn't much like hanging out in the late Mr. Quinn's museum.

"Trace?"

He nearly jumped out of his skin. Skyler was standing over him with two frothy drinks. "I'm sorry. Were you asleep?"

"You walkin' on cat feet?" He glanced down as he reached to meet the glass in her hand halfway. Beautiful bare toes.

"I'm tired of boots." She set her glass on a side table. "Isn't it time you took yours off?"

"I'm afraid to." He was eyeing the drink. It looked like Dairy Queen, but it smelled like booze. Contamination! He glanced up. The anticipation dancing in her eyes mowed down all resistance.

"Well?" she asked hard on the heels of his first taste.

"This isn't something I'd order in public, so it's a treat for sure." He sipped again. "Wow."

"Is that enough kick?"

He chuckled. "I don't think I have to worry about it fillin' out my back pockets. It's going straight to my head."

"Have you been taking those pills?"

"I took one after we ate. Figured the fire would burn up the buzz."

"And the swelling?"

"Seriously, I'll know when I take the boots off.

I hope that's over. I wanna be ready for Cheyenne. Can't miss that one." He patted the space beside him on the sofa. "Neither can you. You've gotta keep taking pictures. Get hooked up with the right kind of media, you'll get your credentials. You gotta prove yourself. That's the way we roll in the PRCA. We don't have tryouts or drafts. You get an amateur permit and you fill it with money. Rodeo's a real sport. No unions, no benefits. Thank God for the Justin Sportsmedicine Teams."

He was talking a mile a minute without missing a move—the way she drew her legs up and tucked them to one side under her bottom without spilling a drop from her full glass. The way she sipped and made herself a little mustache then pressed her lips together and got most of it. But not all. Man, that little sliver of foam would taste good.

He laid his hand on her knee. She was wearing smooth-fitting pants that ended just below where his hand was. Two inches to Skyler skin. He drank deep.

"Yep. Gotta make it to Cheyenne."

"What's so special about Cheyenne?"

"It's a great show. Nice purse. Hometown crowd." He didn't want to sound overly eager, but he felt a crazy itch, worse than skin trapped in a cast. "I want you to be there, Sky. I'm asking you for a date."

She smiled from behind her glass. The foam above her lip taunted him. "Do they have a Ferris wheel?"

"You don't have to ride it. You don't have to ride anything you don't want to."

"I know that. But I want to ride again. I feel safe with you."

"I want you to be safe with me. But not untouched." He leaned over to kiss that sassy bit of foam away, and he bumped into her glass. "Damn." He glanced down. The spill painted a translucent teardrop on her sweet-looking pale orange shirt, smack-dab over her left breast. His eyes lingered—a glance and then some. "Can't talk smooth and make a move at the same time."

"It's washable."

"Let's see." He set his glass aside and leaned over the spill. "Nice top. Kind of a melon color, huh? Or just peachy." He circled the spot with the tip of his nose, tip of his tongue, slippery side of his lip. He took a bit of the cloth between his teeth, sucked on it while he slid his hand from her waist to the underside of her breast. "I'm gonna peel it. Taste the fruit."

She turned to him, straddled him, dropped her head back, lifted her arms as though she'd been cued by some exotic music. He skinned her top over her head, turning it inside out and then tossing it overhead. It opened like a parachute promising a lift, but he had a different conveyance in mind. Her bra gave way easily and flew the way of the parachute. He took full visual measure of her lovely pink-and-white breasts while he shifted beneath her, feeling the pleasure of her weight and her heat and her energy bearing down on his flight deck. He cupped her breasts in his hands and teased her nipples with his thumbs while they kissed hungrily. When he had her nipples standing up hard and tight the way she was doing his penis, he ducked to suckle her, savor her, tease and torture her.

She returned the favor, but all she had to do was ride.

"Ah! You're killin' me, Sky."

She scooted down and unsnapped his jeans. "Lie back and let me finish you off." His zipper gave way to her invading hand. "Inside me."

"No, let me...get..." His hand started for his pocket, but his head knew better. He was unarmored.

And she was hot. Judgment was climbing into the backseat looking for air.

"There's nothing to worry about, Trace," she whispered as he undid her the way she'd undone him. No pausing, no peeking. She was going after his shirt buttons like the thing was on fire.

"You sure?"

"I'm sure."

"I'm a straight shooter, honey, but I don't shoot blanks." And he didn't mind firing off target. *Hardly* minded. Pulling out wasn't his first choice, but he'd do it. He could ask, or he could just do it.

She brushed his bare chest with her breasts and whispered, "How do you know?"

"I'm a cowboy." *Having a cowboy-up moment.* "We're all alike, remember?"

"You're the only cowboy I know. The only one I want to know." She nibbled his nipple while she cosseted his penis between her strong thighs. "Let me know you."

Or he could take her at her word.

She struggled for breath when he found his way inside her. He struggled for control. But he was bent on taking her breath away, and she was determined to claim control. And so the fight was on. He sank into her deeply, and she drew on him thoroughly, and the contest gratified both sides. It was win-win.

They ended up naked and sweaty and basking in wonder. He looked up at the ram's head and smiled. He was something of a leather expert, and he knew for a fact he was making his permanent mark in sweat on the couch. The museum had a new display.

"Does this mean you'll sleep with me?" he asked lazily.

"I already have."

"Not by choice. There was only one bed."

"I knew that going in." She shifted in his arms. "We have several beds here."

"Okay." He combed her hair with his fingers. "Point me to the one you want me in. Given the choice, I'll take a bed over the floor."

"You can take Mike's old room, which is now the guest room, or you can come to bed with me. I sleep in the old guest room. It's free of ghosts."

"Given the choice, I'll take a room that's not haunted."

"You might get more rest if you stay away from me for a while."

He laughed. "What about you?"

"I want to sleep with you. But given the choice, I might not sleep." And neither of them had chosen to make a move yet.

"Is every choice gonna be complicated with you? Because if it is, we can narrow it down to two. Yes or no."

"Yes." She kissed his chin. "I'll go to bed with you."

"Let's get at it." He sat up, taking her with him. "Lead me. Turn your shoulder to me and I'll follow." She tried to turn the tables by slipping her arm around him, but he warned, "Don't try to complicate it."

"I was going to say, *lean on me.*"

"You've heard the term *cowboy up?* That's what I'm doing. I've gotta start putting weight on this thing."

But he was soon limping along, and he thought, *What the hell? Nothing to worry about. Suck up a little sympathy and then suck it up.* "How much farther?"

"Last door on the right."

He put his arm around her. "I'm ready to lean."

"Sometimes a little *cowboy up* goes a long way."

She patted his bare stomach, and it occurred to him that it was a long way to that last door and that the only stitch of covering between them was elastic bandaging and that he was almost sober and that it was all good. Incredibly, ridiculously, unbelievably good.

"How about a shower?" she suggested.

"Sure, I'm game."

"So let's take care of that."

And together they did. They soaped and stroked, kissed and caressed, and if he'd been steady on his feet he would have made love to her under falling water. They toweled each other off and climbed into bed together where he pulled her back against his front and stroked her until she came crying out and quivering and crashing in his hand. She would sleep now, he thought, and he would hold her and breathe her fragrance and listen to her heartbeat.

He would sleep now, she thought.

And she would try to shut her mind down. She'd said he was a good man, which was the kind of observation you could make pretty easily after a day or two, toss it out as a nice thing to say when saying something nice was in order. And they'd had good sex—*really* good sex—between two good people, which probably didn't happen as often as it should. One was bound to be better than the other. Less selfish. More honest. But with Trace, all things were pretty much equal. Two good people. Whatever came of good sex between two good people would have to be a good thing.

But she knew damn well she'd slipped a couple of

notches on the goodness meter. He *could* sleep now. She'd told him there was nothing to worry about. And there wasn't. She wasn't worried. He wasn't worried. Hey, she'd told the truth.

But she hadn't been honest. She couldn't sleep.

And he knew it.

"Skyler?"

"Hmm?"

"What's going on?"

"I'm trying to let you sleep."

"I can feel how hard you're trying." He braced his head in his hand and tried to see what was in her eyes, because they were usually so good at telling tales on her. But not tonight. "What's going on? You don't want to sleep with me?"

"I'm very comfortable with you." She touched his chin with one finger, and then she sighed. "Just not so comfortable with myself."

"I'm listening."

"Well," she said after seemingly endless, ominous silence, "to be honest, I'm not on any kind of birth control."

"Well, uh…neither am I."

"I haven't used any since I got married." Her voice went soft. "I had a miscarriage early on."

The word sounded sad. He knew what it was, but it was way beyond the realm of his experience, and he had no idea what it really meant.

"I'm still listening," he said finally.

"That's it. Those are the simple facts."

"Okay. Now move on to the complicated part." He gave her a good thirty seconds. "That's where I come in."

"I don't want to use birth control. I mean…I wasn't planning for this to happen between us, but it is happening, and it's good, and it feels right." But he felt her stiffen, and that didn't feel right. "I want a baby. I only have half the necessary ingredients."

"Damn." He felt numb. Confused. Broadsided. "What the hell, Skyler? You know, you can buy the other half. I hear you can have it professionally installed."

"I don't like that idea."

He lay back and stared at the ceiling, where moonlight challenged shadows. "You like this one better?"

She came crawling up the side of his chest. "I like *you*, Trace. It feels right to let nature take its course. But you wouldn't have to worry about…"

Another loaded silence.

"About what?"

"Anything. It probably sounds crazy to you. It sounds a little crazy to me, too, and I wasn't trying to trick you. I've never used birth control."

"Never *before*, maybe, but now is *after*. You're lookin' at a new partner here. I figured maybe you were allergic to latex. Or you couldn't get pregnant, and it was hard for you to come out and say it. But I thought that was what you were telling me."

"I don't know for sure. I've had tests. I should be... able."

"Able?" He gave a humorless chuckle. "So you're looking for ready and willing. A proven breeder would be a bonus."

"That sounds bad. Not crazy. *Bad.* But if we didn't know each other, and you were just donating, it would be fine."

"With who?" He shook her off as he jacked himself up on his elbows. "Maybe I don't believe in donating like you don't believe in birth control. When the time comes, yeah, I want kids. Right now I want sex."

"I do, too." Her voice sounded so small, so tragic he almost wanted to take her in his arms.

"This is the damnedest conversation." He carefully swung his legs off the side of the bed, turning his back on her.

"Sometimes I think too much. This wasn't one of those times." She sat up in the middle of the bed and talked to his back. "It's been a long time since I thought about it at all, really. But here we are, and this is a chance. A small chance. If it happened, how would that be a bad thing?"

He turned to her, incredulous. "You didn't ask me."

"But it happens all the time without asking."

"Not to me." He peered at her though the shadows. She was all tousled hair and big eyes. "Look, I don't know anything about my biological father. Isn't that what you call a human breeder? A biological father? Or do you call him a stud? I don't know what else my *biological father* produced. You can't have a proven breeder unless you keep records."

"Oh, Trace, that's not—"

"I don't have a pedigree. I hear you can get something like that when you go to the sperm bank, but me, hell, what you see is what you get." He leaned closer, nose to nose. "Which is why any kid of mine will get to *see* me. Every day, if that's what he wants. Good times, hard times, I'm there. That's what I'm holdin' out for." He lowered his voice. "It's called fatherhood. I know how it works. I learned from the best."

"Is there a chance your father—I mean your biological father—doesn't know about you?"

"Damn good chance. But he didn't stick around to find out, and that's a fact." He grabbed a corner of the bedsheet and pulled it across his lap.

"I wouldn't want you to go away," she said quietly.

"Yeah, but I do go away. A lot."

"I wouldn't ask you for anything, either."

"How about asking me for my kid?"

"Okay."

"What do you mean, *okay?*"

"I mean…okay, can we start over?"

"How do you propose we do that? You haven't been honest with me."

"I am now. I'm being honest with both of us now. Two good people. In the back of my mind, I—"

"You can't push stuff like that into the back of your mind. Like I said, I know how it's supposed to be done. I go by the name my father gave me. Logan had a big ceremony, put on a feed, adopted us the traditional Indian way. Not too long after my mother skipped out on us. He'd already gone through the court, but after she was gone he had this big family thing, so we'd know we were home now. He even gave us Indian names. Two motherless white boys. Well, I guess Ethan's dad was part Indian. Who the hell knows where I came from?"

"Does it matter?"

"Everybody wants to know where they came from, Skyler. You want to know who, and…and why. That's the big one. *Why?*"

He drew a deep breath. He should've been out the door by now, but he realized he was crazy about this woman. He was thinking crazy, feeling crazy. And she was talking crazy to a guy who loved to blow the lid off crazy, but only for eight seconds a pop.

"You should meet him," he said quietly. "Logan. You need to meet my father."

"I know I'd like him."

"Yeah, well, I'm not sure…"

"Not sure he'd like me?"

"What's not to like? You're a woman who knows what she wants, and what she wants is not a bad thing. But I'm not…" He glanced toward the door. He wasn't sure where he should be right now. He knew his wits hadn't been serving him too well in the face of his wants. "What are my other choices again? The ghost's bed or the floor?"

"You stay here," she said as she scrambled toward the edge of the bed. "I know my way around."

"Not around me." She was a slender silhouette standing beside the bed, a shadowy beauty reflected in the mirror on the back of the door, and his hands ached to touch her.

But he shook his head. "You don't know your way around me."

Chapter Seven

Trace looked up from the magazine he was perusing on the kitchen table. "You always sleep this late?"

"No."

Skyler adjusted her wraparound terry-cloth robe. She hadn't expected to be seen in it since nothing had seemed to be stirring. The only sound she'd heard was the regular predawn *coo-OO-oo-woo-woo-woooo* from her resident mourning dove calling his mate. She'd lain in bed listening, imagining Mrs. Dove's tiny heart ticking wildly as she fluffed up the nest. Even if he'd been out all night, who could resist that sweet, plaintive love call? *You always sleep this late?* didn't quite compare, but then Skyler hadn't fluffed or fixed anything, and her tatty robe was no feather dress. She wasn't expecting a love call. She didn't deserve one.

"I mean, it isn't that late, but, yes, it took me a little more time than usual this morning." More explanation than she'd intended, but a simple *no* seemed lonely.

Trace was hat-to-boots dressed, and he'd made his own coffee. Another missed opportunity for a feather. *Damn, he was good-looking.*

"You're leaving?" Of course. Why wouldn't he?

"We're leaving." He closed the magazine. "You're driving."

"How will I get back?"

"You'll figure something out."

"Mike can drive you, and I'll follow."

"Uh-uh. It's over two hours to my place. That's at least an hour and a half longer than I want to spend with your stepson." He sipped his coffee and then gestured with it. "No offense, but he's not that interesting."

"You'd rather spend two hours with me?"

"You're interesting. We haven't had a dull moment yet."

"That's true." He didn't question her willingness to go with him—obviously knew he didn't have to. She wasn't ready to go back to dull moments slowly adding up to dull hours dripping onto the squares of the calendar to form dull days.

"I'll call Mike and tell him to—"

"Forget Mike. Either he'll get his act together here,

or he won't, but you can't do it for him." He stood. "I made coffee."

"I see that. I'll get dressed and make breakfast."

"Make it quick. Goin' down the road, I like to get an early start."

"But I don't want you to have to worry about—"

"I know you don't, Skyler. And now that you've had your come-to-Jesus moment, nobody has to worry. You want a fresh start? You got it. I'll drop you off here on the way back from Cheyenne." He gave her a loaded look. "We have a date for Cheyenne."

She scowled. "That's almost two weeks away."

"I don't know what you think you're gonna do with that horse, but if we take him to my place, I can have you in the saddle by the time we hit the road for Cheyenne." He stepped closer. "I have a spare bedroom. I don't get many guests."

She could hardly breathe. She wanted to go with him, and it scared her. She wasn't afraid of him—he was a little gruff this morning, but he had his reasons, and they were more than halfway reasonable—but the leaving scared her. She might not want to come back, and it would be so easy to, as Trace said, let her wants get ahead of her wits. And then who would she be?

"You know how this is going to play out," she said quietly.

"No, I don't. But I'm into you now, honey, and I'm interested in finding out." He took her shoulders in his hands and looked into her eyes long enough and hard enough to make her tremble inside. "Maybe I'll give you what you want."

"Maybe you already have."

"I doubt it. These things take time." His slight smile did nothing to soften the look in his eyes. "You take the mare to the stud, where he's in his element and he's at his best. And you're right about natural cover. Definitely the way to go, as long as the mare isn't a kicker."

"Trace..."

"And if she is a kicker, a good stud knows how to handle her."

She lifted her hand to push his hat back and touch his four-day-old head wound. "You don't need any more of these."

Four days since they'd met. *Four days.* How could she know anything about him by now?

He smiled, and this time a spark flashed in his eyes. "I've got a hard head."

She could believe that, among other things. When he looked at her with that gleam in his eyes, there were things she knew, and they were sure things, true for the duration of that gleam. True for now, for today. All she wanted was today. They'd agreed to three days, and it was the beginning of day five. She wouldn't think about five rolling into six and seven. Maybe by day nine he would have a gleam in his eye for someone else. The French had it right: c'est la vie.

"You should wear protection," she told him.

"Right." He gave a dry chuckle. "None of that stuff is foolproof."

"There's always a risk, isn't there." Her fingertips disappeared in his hair as she laid her palm against his cheek. "Besides, it takes more than a hat to make a cowboy."

"You believe that or did you get it off a T-shirt?"

She shook her head, laughing. "I don't know what made me think you were all alike."

"Old movies, maybe. Are you gonna get your stuff, or should we just take off before the buzz wears off?"

"Who's buzzed?"

"Come on, woman, we both are. This isn't your first rodeo and it sure as hell ain't mine. Let's see if we can make the whistle."

She took his face in her hands and pulled his head down for a hard and fast kiss. "What's eight seconds in the grand scheme of things?" she proposed.

"Don't knock it. You've seen what I can do in eight seconds."

She grinned. "What about breakfast?"

"We'll stop on the way. Did I tell you I saw a ghost after you left the room last night? She was wearing a crown. Pretty scary. I thought ghosts were white, but this one was yellow. Turned out she was lonely. She asked me for a kiss, so I…" He tucked her hair behind her ear, leaned down and nibbled her neck. "Tasted like sweet creamery butter."

* * *

Skyler had always wondered what it would feel like to act on impulse. Her father had been impulsive, but her mother had planned every day of every life being lived under her roof. Tony had been impulsive, but for a long time she'd called it spontaneity because he was in charge. And then he wasn't. And then she realized he hadn't been, not for a long time. She was saddled with his unkept promises, unpaid debts and his undisclosed loose ends.

There was a bank account she knew nothing about, a woman from Tony's complicated past, a secret gambling history, who knew what else? But now that he was gone, she didn't want to think about it. She didn't want to blame him for it. She'd finished grieving and she might be able to tie up most of the loose ends, but the promises were not hers to keep. And the debts? Michael would have to deal with those if he wanted to keep the business. She loved Michael. She'd raised him—or at least she'd done the part of the job Tony had left for her to do. And while she couldn't undo the spoiled part—couldn't stop him from overestimating the gifts his daddy gave him—she wanted to put what there was in some kind of order and then move on. She wanted to *be ready* to move on.

But for now, she would claim a few days to fill with her own dreams. She grabbed her cameras and a few other necessities and found Trace cleaning up the kitchen from the night before. She'd forgotten about the dishes she'd left in the sink, but he'd rolled up his sleeves and pitched in. She told herself she had nothing to be embarrassed about, but it didn't take.

And he knew it. He turned, drying his hands on a dishtowel, his cowboy hat pushed back from his face, his smile way too cocky for a dishwasher.

"You need to stay off that ankle," she said. "At least until—"

"You're welcome. It was no trouble."

"I forgot about the dishes. Thank you." She gave a tight-lipped smile. "Do you know how adorable you look?"

"Yep."

"May I take a picture?"

"Nope."

"Ooh, with an apron. I actually have one with…"

She started toward a drawer, but he caught her in one damp arm. "That *would* be trouble. You got your stuff together?" She nodded. "Then I'm taking you home with me."

"But I'm driving."

"*This* time."

"And I'm bringing groceries."

"I've got…" He frowned. "I don't know what I've got."

"I know what I've got, and we're taking some along." She nodded toward the pantry. "Fill up a sack with anything that looks good, and I'll get the cooler and unload the fridge."

Trace hesitated. "How about we stop at a store?"

"I *am* a store. Just ask Mike."

He winked at her. "Leave him the enchiladas."

They loaded the pickup and then drove to the corral, where they loaded the horse trailer. Jack went in first. The mustang gave them some trouble, but Trace had a few tricks tucked into his rolled sleeves, and the newly christened Cayenne mellowed out, at least for the moment.

Skyler plugged her cell phone into the dash and punched in a number.

"Hey. I'm taking Trace home."

"In his pickup?" Mike asked sleepily. "You want me to follow you?"

"I want you to take care of things here. Trace has a better setup for getting this horse started, and we really think he's a good prospect. So I might be gone for a few days."

"A few days?"

"That's right. Maybe even longer. I've gotten some good video, and I believe I'm on to something I can develop as a project." No response. "Help yourself in the kitchen." Still no response. "Leftover enchiladas."

With his hat pulled over his eyes, Trace's face was a nose and a smile.

"What kind?"

"Chicken."

"I like beef better."

"Next time. Speaking of beef, we need that head count. Can you get it done today?"

He groaned. "You'll be gone. What difference does it make, today or tomorrow?"

"None. It's up to you, Mike. If you're going to stay in this business, it's time for you to start dealing with..." She glanced at Trace again. He was tilting his seat back, settling in, otherwise occupied. *He'll either get his act together, or he won't.* "You're right. Today, tomorrow, next week, as long as you keep track of the ear tags and figure out what's missing."

"It's not just *my* business. We'll get that all straightened out, Skyler. It should all be fifty-fifty."

"I'm not worried about that right now. Call my cell if you need anything."

She ended the call and started the pickup.

"I have total cell-signal protection at my place," said the voice under the hat. "But Mike's got my phone number." He thumbed his hat back and gave her a knowing look. "If he needs anything."

"Gotcha." She slowed at the gate, and the pickup rumbled over the cattle guard. "Any day now it's going to sink in that things have changed, and when it does, it's going to hit him hard."

"Maybe it's time for you to stand back and let that particular signal get through."

"He should have his turn at the ZQ wheel." She glanced over her shoulder at the sign as they pulled onto the highway. ZQ Ranch. A. R. Quinn. "Maybe he can make it pay. His grandparents built the place, and his father did well with it for a long time. They say ranching is in the blood."

"They say that about everything. The big question is, is that what he wants?"

"It's what he inherited." She shrugged. "He really thinks he's kept things going and somehow it hasn't been all that tough. I've tried to get him to pay attention to the bottom line, but he just can't find his way down there. He likes clouds." Out of habit she kept an eye on the fence line and what could be seen of the pasture from the road. "And the ZQ is earthbound."

"How about you? You like clouds?"

"Who doesn't? They make pictures in the sky. I love making pictures." At the moment the eastern sky was clear, and the air was cool. "When you're a kid you try to get the window seat on a flight so you can look down at them, and you imagine getting out and playing on them, like they do in cartoons." She turned a quick smile on her copilot. "I haven't always been afraid of heights."

"I don't fly," he said. "Too risky."

"So you're earthbound." She frowned. "But you don't ride with a helmet."

"Hell, no. That's for bull riders. I ride broncs. I'm a *real* cowboy. You pay your money, you choose your limb." He chuckled. "On the tree of life."

"I guess so." But she couldn't let it go completely. "You really should wear a protective vest."

"You really should take another look at your protection priorities." He gestured, a two-handed holdup.

"Okay, full disclosure. I have a vest, but I don't always wear it. Gets in the way sometimes."

"Full disclosure?" She couldn't help smiling.

"You like that one?"

"Not really, but I appreciate the effort."

"Close but no cigar?" He grinned.

"You did *not* say that."

"Hell, I don't even know what it means. Something bad?" He shifted in her direction, his eyes full of mischief. "Close to what?"

"I think it has something to do with—"

"Damn if she doesn't have an answer. Trains?"

"Games."

"That makes sense. Games of chance, right?"

"Carnival games."

The kind she was good at. Give it the right spin and take home a prize. This verbal roller coaster was something he was proving to be good at, and she risked her dignity by going along for the ride. But he was worth it.

"Where do they have you playing for cigars?"

"They used to, back in the day. Swing the hammer, ring the bell, win a cigar. But you never quite reach the bell, so the carny shouts—"

"Close, but no cigar," he barked theatrically. "How do you know these things?"

"I've been to a lot of fairs."

"Yeah, but princesses don't swing hammers."

"Princesses do what they're told. You might as

well study up and do *whatever* better than the next girl."

"Close, but no cigar," he said quietly.

Always thinking. Nothing cliché about this cowboy. She could hear the gears whirring inside his head. Cigars were a joke. They were also a gift, a celebration, a recognition and a tradition. They were all over the map, and so was Skyler. And she knew it. He'd said he was into her—whatever that meant—so he might as well know it, too. She was a perfectly serviceable instrument slightly out of tune.

"I like my pink rabbit's foot," he said. And then he drifted off.

She attended to the road signs and the mile markers. Newcastle wasn't far from the South Dakota state line, but she wasn't sure how far Trace's place was from Newcastle. She waited as long as she could, but eventually she had to wake him up to find out.

"We're gonna turn left up here," he said, leaning forward in his seat as though he were pouring on the gas. "Say goodbye to the beaten path."

Beaten was right. They'd gone from interstate to battered two-lane county asphalt. A stretch of gravel parted the grassland down the middle and pointed the way toward pine-covered foothills. Another turn led to a hill, a sweeping valley and two log structures that looked as though they'd been planted rather than built amid the pines.

The house was small but brawny-looking with its dark, rough-hewn cedar bones and its white chinking.

The big barn with its gambrel roof was surrounded by weathered corrals. Nothing was painted, but it didn't have to be. The materials had been borrowed from the surroundings and had stood the test of considerable time, but they made no sore thumbprint. One day the earth would welcome them back.

Skyler pulled up to the corral gate as wordlessly instructed. She watched Trace in the towing mirror and followed his hand signals precisely. She recognized an immediate *whoa* when she saw one, and an O with three finger feathers read like a gold star. The trailer was set, and the two horses were soon racing the length of a narrow paddock while Trace pumped water into a metal tank.

"You're a helluva driver, J.J."

"J.J.? What happened to *Sky?*"

"Have I called you Sky?" He looked up, adjusting his hat against the sun. "Skyler's a pretty name. I've never met one before."

"Who's J.J.?"

"Burt Reynolds in *Smokey and the Bandit,* one of Logan's favorite movies. A good cook is Doris, and a good driver is J.J."

"What about a bronc rider?"

"That was a J.W. until I saw *J. W. Coop.* That's another one Logan had in his video collection, but he'd forgotten about the cowboy's crazy mother. Said all he remembered was the bronc riding. But he let that particular handle go by the wayside, and now an up-and-coming bronc rider is another Trace Wolf

Track—" he slipped his arm around her shoulders "—who likes to call for the gate and reach for the Sky."

She smiled and pressed her fist against his shoulder. "Now I know how you work those arms in the off-hours."

"Soon as we get electricity out here I'll probably lose my edge." He saw her surprise and laughed. "Did you think you were getting a free stay at some gentrified dude ranch?"

"I thought…" She pointed to a power pole. "Isn't that electricity?"

"Hell, that's a yard ornament." He nodded toward the far side of the outbuildings. "That's the round pen, there. I built that myself." It was made of cedar boards. Other than repairs, it was the only recent construction on the place. "That's the beginning of my training facility. I'm a year or so out from an indoor arena."

"How far from indoor plumbing?"

He looked into her eyes, shook his head and laughed again.

She had no idea what was so funny. "I'm not complaining, mind you. Just asking. How long have you been here?"

"I found this place two years ago. Been vacant for quite a while, so I got it pretty cheap. It's hard to find a piece of land in this state that isn't being tapped for oil or fracked for gas. I like my well water straight up." He tucked his thumbs into the front pockets of his jeans. "The house has its rough edges. It's pretty old, but it's solid. Worth saving."

"And it all fits together. What do you use for heat?"

He jacked up one eyebrow. "Love."

"Oh, good," she quipped. "Too bad it's summer."

"I'm countin' on global warming." He pointed past the round pen toward a grassy slope. "Buck-and-pole fence. You like that?"

"Love that," she said of the rustic wood fence that ran up and over the hill.

"See, that's how it works. All you need is love."

"Nobody loves a big tease."

"Who told you that? Your mama?"

"Probably." *Remember, Skyler, the girl who teases never pleases.* "I can't always tell when you're putting me on."

"That's what makes it fun. You've had a little fun with me, too." He gave her a firm squeeze. "Come on, admit it."

"I'm only a little bit of a tease."

"Which leaves the door open, doesn't it?" He winked at her.

"This much." She measured an inch between thumb and forefinger. "Seriously."

"That's enough to keep me from ever knowing for sure. Which makes things interesting." His arm slid away from her, and the playfulness faded from his eyes as he turned his attention to the weathered pine poles that lined up end to end and meandered through green needlegrass and blue grama dappled with clumps of silvery sage. "A couple of spans need replacing on the east side. I ran out of poles and strung up some wire, but that's temporary. I'm always working on something."

"It never ends," she said, feeling strangely bereft. "But think of the pictures we'll get here."

"You think about the pictures. I'm thinking about training a horse."

She helped him unload groceries in the sunny, farmhouse-style kitchen, which was as tidy as she should have imagined after he'd shown his true colors by cleaning up her dishes. It was also plumbed and wired. The appliances and the tile floor were new, the pine cabinets rustic and the countertop was faded Formica. There was a pine table with chairs at both ends and benches along the sides—furniture that might have come with the house.

He noticed her taking stock, and he smiled. "We never did stop for breakfast, did we?"

"I didn't want to wake you up." She nodded toward the cooler sitting in the middle of the floor. "I brought eggs and milk. Do you like French toast?"

"I like everything."

She smiled. "You'll have to show me how to turn on the love light for the stove."

"You want me to bring your bag in first?"

"I want you to take your boots off and put your feet up."

"I want you to forget about my feet. They're not my best feature." He set the cooler on the counter next to the refrigerator. "And you don't need to be cookin' all the time, Doris. Just relax and be Skyler."

"I like to cook." She laughed as he slid her a squint-eyed glance, unconvinced. "Don't worry. The only Cayenne I brought is the horse."

"Make yourself comfortable. I'll get the rest of your stuff."

The fieldstone fireplace took up a whole wall in the living room, which was sparely furnished with couch and one easy chair. A braided rug covered much of the pine floor, and the heavily chinked log walls were undecorated. The view from the large window was all the decor a cowboy probably needed. Beauty abounded here. Trace's land was surrounded by well-dressed mountains.

"It needs a lot of work."

"You can't improve on that," she said of the views. She hadn't heard him coming up behind her. "And I love the house. You can't get this kind of character in new construction. I know that from experience."

"You have a nice house."

She looked up as he came to stand at her shoulder, and then back to the mountain. Trace had better mountains. This was the back side of the Black Hills. "It was supposedly built for me, but I didn't get much input. He'd always been planning to build a bigger house, and he never said as much, but I think Mike's mother was in on the planning."

"What would you change?" He laid his hand high on her back. "Besides one of the bedrooms."

"There wasn't much furniture when I came along. Within the first few years I managed to make the place at least half mine."

"Not the half with the dead heads on the walls, I'm guessing."

She feigned surprise. "You wouldn't take me for a hunter?"

"I'll take you for who you are, woman. I say *woman.* You could be a hunter, sure. But you didn't…" He looked down at her quizzically. "Are you?"

"I've hunted." *Squeeze, don't pull. Take the shot. Now, Skyler, take the shot.* "I've never hit anything."

He nodded thoughtfully. "Did you want to?"

"I was hunting. Of course I wanted to hit something." One of the somethings appeared in her mind. Her closest call. "But I didn't want to kill her. Or injure her. So I just scared her."

"What happens when you shoot at a target? The red-and-white kind."

She looked up grinning. "Bull's-eye."

"That's what I figured. I've hunted, too, and I'm not a bad shot. Ethan could shoot the pink eye out of a white rabbit half a mile away during a blizzard."

"Eww."

"But Logan was the one who brought home the meat." He lifted one shoulder. "We gotta eat, right? But we don't have to hang the leftovers on the wall."

"You have your trophies," she reminded him indignantly.

"Yeah, I know. Question is, where are they?" He made a pretense of looking around. "So, what would you change about ZQ Ranch if you ever got around to it?"

"The feel of the place, I guess. I should clear out all the leftovers. The arsenal, the toy trains, the fishing tackle, the trophies. Mine, too. I've never wanted them on display, but my husband was big on displays."

"I didn't see anything with your name on it." She gave him a questioning glance. "Yeah, I looked."

"You don't believe I was ever Princess Kay of the Milky Way?"

"I figured you were putting me on with that one. Just a little tease. Is that a real title?"

"It certainly is. My parents had a very small dairy farm in Minnesota. My mother had much bigger dreams."

"And your father?"

"My father had a very small dairy farm in Minnesota."

"Are they still—"

"No. They went under." Under the influence, under the weather and finally under the gun. She shook her head quickly. "I had no trouble giving away clothing. My husband was a collector of hats and boots, and Mike had no use for them, so we gave them away. Boxes of brand-new hats and boots. A thrill for Goodwill, let me tell you."

"Hey, if Mike wants to keep the trains…"

"They really weren't Mike's trains. Mike never cared for them. I should've taken you downstairs and showed you the train room. It's out of the way, and I wouldn't know how to begin to take it apart." She smiled, remembering. "He hired a master carpenter to build the foundation and brought in a hobbyist from Denver to help lay the track and set up all the miniatures."

"Must've been an expensive proposition."

"I'm sure it was. That was before he got sick. Before I took over the bookkeeping." She turned back to the window. "He loved his trains."

"And you loved…"

"Horses. I've had some *beautiful* horses. I have trophies for those, too."

"Where are they?"

"In boxes. I sold all my horses." She looked up at him. "Is there a secondary market for trophies with other people's names on them?"

"Probably," he said with a smile. "If the name is Elvis or Princess Diana."

"Wrong princess."

"Not my type." He squeezed her shoulder. "I have a couple of nice saddle horses. Care to go for a ride?"

"Not as long as you're still limping."

"I won't be limping. I won't be walking. That's what the horse is for." He stepped away. "You don't have to take care of me, woman. I'm a grown-up."

"Why do you call me *woman?*"

"Let me think. Why do I…" He folded his arms. "Let me look at you while I think. Oh, man. Man, oh, man." He thought for a moment and shook his head. "Nope, that doesn't work for me. *Woman, oh, woman.*" He grinned. "You make my heart sing."

He directed her to his tack room in the barn, offered her Jack with a nod and told her to saddle up. She met him at the gate. He was riding a beautiful dark bay Arab mare bareback.

"I could have done that, too," she informed him.

"Any way you want it, baby."

"I prefer *woman.*"

"See there? I knew that. I was just testing." He kept his seat while he leaned way over the horse's side to close the gate behind them. "I'm not showboating. Can't handle the stirrup right now. When we get back home I'm gonna break out the wobble board I scored from a physical therapist the last time around and see how much it hurts to wobble."

"That doesn't sound like the best idea, b—"

"Don't say it. We just put *baby* on the censorship list." He clucked for an easy trot. "Along with *boy* and… What else? *Bitch.* And *bitchin'.* Hate that one."

"I was going to say *but.* With one *t. But* I'm sure

you know what you're doing, having injured many of your best features."

"No, I haven't. Not the one with the two *t*'s. That's prime cut."

"For now. Wait till you're looking at the next ten-year hill."

"Here's lookin' at you looking at the next hill." He saluted her. "You wanna crawl up the side or take it head-on?"

She dug in her heels and cried, "Ballin' the jack!"

And she took off like a shot. There was nothing better than a good race. But her head start was for naught. She heard the Arab closing in, felt them breeze past and take the hill, and admired their ascent to the top. She remembered reading that the bareback event required the greatest athleticism of all rodeo events, and seeing Trace ride effortlessly bore out that claim.

"Told you Jack wasn't born to run," he called out triumphantly as she topped the hill on the losing horse.

The mare had barely broken a sweat. "What's her name?"

"Teabiscuit." She laughed, and he added, "Seriously."

"Oh, man." She shook her head as the horses fell into a walk, side by side. "For a good time, call Trace Wolf Track."

"I don't give out my number. I like to make the calls myself. I'm old-fashioned that way."

"Will I get one?"

He reached for her hand. "You'll get more than that if you play your cards right."

"Play yours right and I might answer." She gave a sassy smile. "I have caller ID."

"I'm unlisted." He winked at her. "Two savvy players make an interesting game."

"You're more fun than a county fair." She was pretty sure she'd never held hands with another rider, but she could get used to it, she decided. The wink, too.

"Is that a good thing?"

"A very good thing." She drew on his hand, and he leaned offside again, clearly feeling another good thing coming. And that was her kiss.

Chapter Eight

Cayenne took to the round pen like salt to a wound at first. He burned it up. But he quickly settled into the notion that Skyler was playing with him and the longe line they were attaching for the first time to one of Trace's hand-tied rope halters was one of her toys. He liked the circle better than the square, and Skyler soon shared his preference. She felt the connection she'd known from the beginning with this horse, but now it traveled back and forth along a smooth braided rope.

"You have to win him over by winning," Trace cautioned her. "But you want him to enjoy the game. He loves to move. Teach him to move on your terms."

"Do you really think I'll be able to back him before we go to Cheyenne?"

"You'll back him before we saddle him," he told her. "You'll know when it's time."

Supper was a simple soup-and-sandwich fare, and afterward they made a production of unveiling Trace's ankle. The mottled bruising was proclaimed a work of art. He put a CD into his living room sound system and tested his range of motion on the exercise disc, rotating slowly, rocking gingerly, wincing generously, cowboying up without much cussing. He obviously had more than a nodding acquaintance with a therapeutic wobble board.

"I always start with Willie Nelson," he confided when she offered her shoulder as a stabilizer. "He takes care of all the whining for me. If I was alone, I'd whine along with him."

"Please don't let me put a crimp in any part of your therapy."

"No, I'm doing fine. I don't feel sorry for myself." With his hands resting on Skyler's shoulders, Trace rolled the ball underfoot, alternating weight on, weight off for short intervals. Standing still, she felt like the reluctant partner in the dance couple. He smiled. "I've got your full attention."

When he'd had all the exercise he could take, he asked her to help him rewrap his ankle. Again, he knew what he was doing. He gave Logan credit for turning him on to the witch hazel he used on his bruises, and he praised his friend Hank Night Horse for teaching him the varieties and the wonders of elastic-bandage wrap. She learned all about figure eights and stirrups that had nothing to do with horses, about compression bandaging and basket weaving and how to work with all kinds of elastic and adhesive and tape that wasn't really tape. And after he pronounced it a job well-done, he offered "spirits for the spirited."

"I don't have any brandy," he said. "Or ice cream. But I remember you like your whiskey straight up."

"I don't like whiskey at all." She smiled, recalling the two drinks she'd knocked back within moments of meeting him that first night. "That was for show."

"Well, that was impressive." He braced his hands on his knees, ready to try out his new footwear—the bandage and a white tube sock constituting a pair. "I'd suggest a walk in the moonlight, but there's no moon, and my stride is way off. We could play cards for real. Or checkers. Or we could make out here on the sofa."

"What about TV?" She glanced at the shelving unit, where a small one was tucked in with the music system.

"You've got two channels to pick from on a good night, but that could be the lead-in to making out on the sofa." He squinted menacingly. "And don't try anything funny. I have a box of condoms in every room."

"You must entertain a lot."

"Not here. This is my sanctuary." He leaned back, stretching out his wings along the top of the backrest.

"While you were cleaning up in the kitchen I went around spreadin' the love just for you."

"We're safe, then. All the bases are covered."

He stared at her for a moment, finally shook his head. "Why do I feel guilty? Like I'm holding out on you or something."

"You really know how to spoil the mood. I thought cowboys were supposed to be sort of love 'em and leave 'em."

He kept staring, as though he was considering options that could set a definitive course. He moved suddenly, knelt in front of the side table, opened a drawer and pulled out a box. "Come on. Let's go."

"Where?"

"Kitchen table. That's what I always use."

"Oh. I thought you said…"

"You got a better idea?"

"I don't want to, um…"

"You don't wanna play with me anymore? I'm not the cowboy you thought I was? Cut the crap, Skyler." He tossed the box on the pine coffee table.

Bicycle.

"And cut the cards. I'm pullin' out all the stops, woman. I'll beat you every hand."

"I think I'll take that whiskey," she said, non-plussed.

He limped into the kitchen and came back with a bottle and two short glasses.

"What are we playing for?" She started to move so he could have the sofa.

"Well, let's see. *No, sit.* Do you smoke?" He sat on the floor across from her and poured two drinks. "You can't win, but you get close enough, I might let you have the prize. Horseshoe rules."

"Horseshoe?"

"Close," he said. "Close counts in horseshoes. Try to keep up, Sky. The stakes are high."

He won the first three hands of whist, but she took the next two. She would never know whether he threw the two after that, nor would she care. She loved winning. It made her feel flush and fierce. But all the posturing went by the wayside when he finished his drink, got up without a word and disappeared down the dark hall. She waited for a sound or a sign, but she heard nothing except cricket music outside the open window.

She hadn't paid much attention to anything but the bathroom when he'd first shown her down the hall. "I'll put your bag in here," he'd said, and she'd noted that *here* was the door across the hall from the one she was looking for. She skipped that door now. All four doors along the narrow passage stood open to darkness. She chose the one at the end and whispered his name as she entered.

He came to her, took her face in his hands and took possession of her mouth with a resolute, probing kiss. She clutched him to her, spreading her hands wide on his back and taking the measure of its size and shape and might. She kept her hands tight and took the tapered path to the small of his back, where she found more of the same—smooth skin over solid muscle.

Her discovery made him groan with pleasure. The sound of his name was all he needed to hear. He wanted her with him in the same sweet way—uncovered and unfettered—and he had to steady himself in the face of the wildness that threatened to overtake him. He took care in peeling away her clothing, unbuttoning and unzipping even as he saw himself tearing the stuff off and kicking it away. When it was gone he lifted her in his arms and kissed her breasts. She wrapped her legs around his waist and he felt the intimate touch of hair and moist folds of flesh and welcome and trust, all pressed against his stomach and ripe for the taking.

There would be no falling to the floor, no making do with the sofa, no repurposing the kitchen table. He wanted her in his bed—*his* bed—and he wanted her now, and then again, and long into the night, and slow and easy in the morning.

She rode him hot and hard, and he held her hips in his hands and bucked up to meet her as she drove down, moved as slow and deep as she could take, would take, stroking her inside and out until she quivered, cried out for him, called his name, screamed his name, whispered his name as she sank down, down, down into his arms and shed warm tears against his chest.

He didn't ask her why, but he asked himself why he would have joined her if tears were part of his nature. Maybe it was for the coupling of their bodies, the sheer power of one against one and one with one. Maybe it was for the way it happened, the beauty, the hazard of it, or for the small coupling that would not happen inside her and away from him. Not tonight. He wasn't kidding about the box of condoms in every room.

She probably wept for her confusion and for his. He had little experience with a woman's tears. But, then, he'd had no experience with a woman like Skyler.

"Tell me something about your husband," he said quietly when they lay side by side in the cool night air.

"What?"

"Something that'll tell me who he was. I feel like I came into your life at the wrong time. Like you're still with somebody else."

"I'm not with anyone else." The first words were raspy. She cleared her throat and added, "I'm on my own."

He was nothing if not persistent. "Tell me *one thing* about your husband." Patient, but persistent.

"I'm here with you, Trace. We're making—"

"One telling thing."

He felt no resistance in her silence. She was trying to come up with the right thing to say. The honest and honorable thing.

"He was a good man." Her chuckle sounded hu-morless, and he thought it might be the effect of the darkness or the cool air. "That's what they all say, isn't it?"

"All who?"

"Eulogists." She paused. "But he *was* a good man. He was *take-charge Tony*."

"Was that his name?" Of course it was. The sound of it chilled him, and he drew the bedsheet around his shoulders. "Logan doesn't name the dead. He's very traditional." He listened to the steady sound of her breathing. He wasn't ready for her to go to sleep. "But I don't have a problem with it. Do you?"

"It's only been a year."

"In my father's house, that's when you put on a feed in their honor and wipe the tears away. The Lakota have a ceremony for everything."

"And you—"

"Tell me something else, Skyler. Help me know him."

"Why?"

"Because I'm…" He found her hand lying between them, and he took it in his. "Don't think too much. Just tell me." *Tell me what I'm up against.*

"We had two marriages."

"You mean *he* had two marriages."

"I'm not thinking too much, so I said what I meant." She drew his hand to her lips and kissed him as if to reassure him or thank him. Quiet him, maybe. "You're playing the grief counselor, right? At first I liked playing May to his September. But I moved on to June, July, August, and he still wanted

May. He wanted the girl who looked up to him and smiled prettily and never doubted." She sighed. "Logan's right. I shouldn't talk about him now."

"You're not talking about him. You're talking about you."

"Well, then, that's fair, isn't it? He's not here."

"Yeah, he is."

"Maybe you're right. A year isn't enough."

"I didn't say that." He groaned. "Hell, what do I know?"

"Good question." She shifted toward him. "Tell me something about your mother."

Damn. The woman knew how to aim. "She's dead to me."

"What do you remember?"

He was thinking, trying to remember what the woman even looked like. It was a strange thing to do, given the effort he'd spent in forgetting. Long ago he'd stopped wanting her around him, so why call up memories of her and run the risk of speculation, which was a ticket that had *frustration* printed right across the middle.

"What's her name?" Skyler asked softly.

"Tonya. Her name was Tonya. And what I remember is she left us."

"And you never heard from her."

"Yeah, we did." And, yeah, it was coming back. As if he needed this. But to be fair, he'd started it. "She called a few times and made promises. I told her I wasn't goin' with her. No way. I was done with her kind of life."

"It wasn't the first time?"

"Hell, no. She left Ethan and me alone for three days once. I think it was three days. Maybe it only seemed like…" He drew a deep breath, wishing he could tell it without calling it all back up in his head. "I know it was two nights. Two really long nights."

"How old were you?"

"Old enough to make baloney sandwiches and keep the door locked. We were living in, uh…" Which crappy shoebox? Which windowless pit? "Down south someplace. Alabama, or Texas, maybe. It was hot. I remember that." He tried to think of something funny about those years. Something tasty and easy to swallow. "I used to have an accent when I was a kid."

"You still do. A little bit."

"Nah, this haint nuthin'. I had a real drawl back then. Got rid of it purdy damn quick when I moved to Indian country. They like to tease the daylights out of you."

"That's where you learned it."

"Had to. Glad I did. It's funnern' hell. You think I'm any good at it?"

"Oh, yes. If they gave teaser trophies, you'd be a sure winner."

"I'd put it front and center, too. Set it in the middle of the table and fill it with flowers. Logan would love that." And Trace was breathing easy again.

"I feel as though I know him. You've drawn me a picture of a wonderful man. Why can't I do that? You know, for Tony."

"He left you alone, and you're mad at him for it."

"He died," she insisted. "He didn't run off."

"He left you alone. You took care of him, tried to keep him around, but he left anyway."

"He *died*." The word seemed to bounce around in the dark. They listened to it ping-pong, loathe to pile on another troublesome word until that one settled. "It was almost…a relief."

"I know. Not to have to worry anymore, wondering what's gonna happen tomorrow. All at once you're free. You're alone, still not sure what's gonna happen, but you feel like the worst must be over. There's peace in the valley."

"It's not the same, Trace."

"Maybe not. But I know what it's like to feel a little guilty over that relief."

"Does it go away?"

"Yeah. It does." He stroked the back of her hand with his thumb. "And like you said, your husband died. No choice about leaving, and he can't come back. When I say my mother's dead to me, it's not because I'm angry. It's because I've let it go, and I don't want her back."

"And you're not alone. In your life, I mean."

"I'm not?" He chuckled. "No buffalo roaming

around here, but I've got the deer and the ante-lope."

"You searched long and hard for a place like this."

"Yes, I did."

And he wanted to share it with someone. Some-day. Once he'd followed the road to the pot of gold, made his mark in a young man's game before it took a crippling toll on his body. He wanted it all, and he wasn't going to let one dream step on the other. He'd told Skyler his wants had gotten ahead of his wits, and maybe that was even truer than he'd realized. His heart had gotten in on the act before he was ready. But the heart—the way it worked hard if not tirelessly and kept on working from start to finish—maybe the heart was always ready. *Ready when you are, slowpoke.*

"I'll say this—somebody's depending on you, you gotta be there. That's the way I was raised. By my father."

"Not all mothers…"

"I know that, Skyler. Like you, for example. You took on a motherless kid, and you stuck by him."

"I married his father."

"Yeah. I hear that can work."

"*Work* is the operative word," she said. "Two will-ing partners. Maybe one more willing than the other at times, but it turns out there are so many more considerations than you anticipate when you take those lovely vows. The considerations are right there in the words, and you say them, but you have to live with them for a while before you know what they mean."

"Which is why kids shouldn't get married."

"I wasn't a kid."

"I didn't mean you. I meant the guy who played with the toy trains."

She laughed. "You're jealous!"

"I am not. I just wish I'd found you first."

"Let's see, you would've been about…"

"Don't you dare go there." It was his turn to laugh. "Look, it's a stupid way to feel, but guys aren't the brightest bulbs on the planet. I'm not supposed to say that out loud, but we all know it's true.

"I've got this image of you tied to the tracks and me coming to the rescue." He let go of her hand so he could draw her a picture overhead. He used both hands, big dusky shadows in the starlit room. "Little tiny you, little tiny me, little tiny train on the table some carpenter built." He spread his hands wide. "Big man runnin' the transformer, setting the dial for ballin' the jack."

They laughed together, and he realized how very funny laughter sounded in the dark, and how it fed on itself and bred more laughter.

And when it died down and the silence rushed in to fill the space, the thoughts came back, which gave rise to words made weighty by darkness.

"Life seems so disjointed sometimes," she said.

"Just when you think you know where you're going, you come to another unmarked crossroads. I don't know where I'm going now, but I know I'm going to be a mother. A good one. My baby will be the light of my life. I promise you that."

"My kid will have a father," he said. "I promise him that."

They worked Cayenne together for most of the next morning. When they came in for lunch, Skyler fell asleep on the sofa. She woke up staring at a rough-hewn beam in an unfamiliar ceiling. It took a moment to climb out of her sleep hole, the place she fell into whenever she slept during the day. It was an unsettling place to find herself in. She wasn't a nap-taker, and she didn't *fall* asleep as a rule. She *went* to sleep.

Trace's place. Ah, yes, she was in a good place.

She padded to the kitchen in her stockinged feet and called his name, but there was no answer. She heard a breeze swishing through the junipers outside and a woodpecker making its mark, but no trace of Trace except the sandwich he'd left on a plate and an apple on a note.

Sky—
I took the pickup. If you feel like it, mount up
and follow the fence over the hill. You might
catch me working.
Trace

She ate the sandwich because he'd made it for her, and she took the apple and her camera bag to the bench by the back door, where she sat down, put on her boots and surveyed the tidy kitchen. Plate. She washed and dried her plate, and then she hurried to the corral to find that he'd brought Jack in from the pasture and had him waiting to do her bidding.

She was busy hauling up on the cinch, glanced over Jack's back and saw Cayenne checking them out from the other side of the fence. He was communing more with Jack than with her, but he knew she was there. She could feel his awareness of her. Not as wary as he once was, but still uncertain of her makeup. She slipped her camera out of the bag she'd hooked over the saddle horn and snapped a picture of gentle and wild, nose to nose. Jack, the blazed-face sorrel, and Cayenne, the red-faced, red-peppered gray, were as close as they appeared to be, and they knew it. Take away the fences, Trace had reminded her, and they would fly away and never look back.

Trace reminded her of a lot of things. Winning and losing, beginning and ending, hurting and healing came to mind. Something was different about the last pair. She'd have to think about it when she got around to thinking again. For now, she was doing what came naturally. She mounted up.

The buck-and-pole trail led her to the top of the hill, and from there she saw a most glorious sight—a working man. He was beautifully buff and bare to the waist, his chambray shirt flapping in the breeze from the top of the A-frame buck that had lost its poles.

She took a few pictures, put the camera away and started down the hill. Trace hadn't seen her yet. The pickup tailgate was down, and she saw a couple of new twelve-foot poles, a chain saw and a big wooden box like the one her father had kept in the barn. Nails, bolts, tools, the increasingly present pint. "Sippin' whiskey," he'd called it. And she'd shrugged off her sinking feeling and saddled her horse.

Trace wielded a mallet over the junction of span and brace, striking his target with every swing. His shoulders glistened in the sun. Skyler was going to descend on him like a thing with feathers. She nudged Jack's flanks with her boot heels and imagined herself flying down the slope. The best way to fly was on horseback, the wind filling her hair like a sail. He snatched his hat off and waved at her. Waved her off? Did he think she was going to—

Whoa!

Jack went down on his knees, scrambled back up and took a couple of stumbling sidesteps. Skyler dismounted as soon as the horse had his footing. Wild-eyed, snorting, he pranced in place, tethered by her hold on the reins. He was calmed by her voice, but he balked at her attempt to check his legs. She waited, apologizing and reassuring until the horse accepted her hand on his neck. He was okay.

"You must've been born in the saddle," Trace said quietly.

She turned, startled, which seemed a little crazy, considering the surprise she'd just had. Then she realized she was quaking inside. Aftershock.

Trace was tucking his leather work gloves into his back pockets. "I've never seen a tighter seat. By all rights you should've sailed over his head."

"By all rights he should've thrown me. But he kept us both…" She drew a slow, tremulous breath. "What was it? A trench?"

"Tried to warn you. Prairie-dog holes. Weren't there last time I was up here. Got some huntin' to do." He kicked at the loosened dirt surrounding another trap. "You okay? Scared me spitless."

"Us, too." Her voice had gone squeaky, but she managed a shaky smile. "Stupid move."

He stepped up and took her in his arms. "Is this what you were looking for?"

His skin was warm and damp, his arms blessedly powerful. Why *blessedly* she couldn't say. Her legs were just as damn powerful as his arms were. But her insides took the *settle down* cue from the rock-solid feel of him.

"You wanna buck one out in Cheyenne?"

"No, thanks."

"Let you wear my vest," he offered.

That wouldn't do it. Not if she was pregnant. And she could be, just might possibly be. The beginning of the very thing she wanted most might have been here and gone inside of a few days, and she'd have nothing to show for it other than a little blood.

She held Trace tighter.

"Hey." He leaned back and looked down at her. "Are you hurt?"

Damn her silly nerves, she was *crying*. She shook her head furiously.

"Just a little delayed heebie-jeebies?"

She nodded and pressed her forehead to his shoulder. "My car almost got hit by a train once. Felt like a bullet whizzed past my head."

"Damn trains."

She took a swipe at her hot tears with the back of her wrist. She was still holding one end of the split rein, which meant she wasn't a total failure. "I'm being silly again. Jack's the one who…"

"He's fine. Look at him. Steady as a rock."

Trace got her to take notice of the horse, already looking for grass. *If we're just gonna stand here, I might as well be eating.* She sniff-giggled like a six-year-old who'd fallen off a swing.

"Jack, you're a keeper," Trace called out to the horse. Jack was nosing around, picking over the possibilities. "That's the way I'll advertise him," he confided. "Did you hit pretty hard?"

She swallowed. "I think I bit my tongue." And she grimaced. "I taste blood."

"Open your mouth."

He ducked, peered, nodded. "It's a gusher. You want me to kiss it better?"

"Would you?"

He lowered his head and applied several soft,

gentle kisses to her lips. Her tongue didn't get into the action, but she had the feeling he would not have recoiled no matter what shape it was in. This cowboy was a keeper, but Skyler would keep that to herself.

"How's your foot?"

"It's giving me passable understanding." He bent to pick up the loose rein and hand it to her. "Long as I don't stand on it too long."

"What can I do to help?" she asked as she took care of securing Jack to the fence.

"Almost got it licked. Can you hold a pole for me?"

"Just hold it?"

"That's all I need." He laid his hand on her arm before he put on his second glove. "You sure you're okay? You still seem a little shaky."

"I thought that was the idea." She offered a tentative smile. "Isn't that… I pride myself on my pole work." The surprise in his eyes bucked her up. "I took lessons."

He laughed. "I can function with a bum leg, but if I slip and smash a finger, it's all over. It all starts with the hands."

"I know. So please be careful."

"Let's see…" Trace made a production of eyeballing Skyler's height and the fallen end fence rail for placement on the buck. "What's the best way for you to do this? You could get underneath, but I'm not sure you can bear the weight. And you're a straddler, aren't you?"

She smiled a little more. "I like to ride."

"Well, throw your leg over and get behind me. This baby's gonna get nailed good this time."

Skyler held the pole while Trace pounded the spike. "Hey, guess what," she shouted at his back. "We're riding the rail!"

Trace lay on his back in the grass with his legs propped up on the A-frame buck, bad ankle crossed over the good one. He'd put his shirt back on, but he'd left it open because it was hot out, and he was hot, and he'd noticed her taking notice of him, so he thought he'd keep her options open. He knew what he had going for him, and he figured he might as well use it.

He'd covered his eyes with his hat, balanced the front of the sweatband on the bridge of his nose so he could see her sitting up there on the rail they'd hung together. She was wearing a battered straw hat, but he was pretty sure her face and her arms and her chest, even the top part of her breasts, were going to be red tonight. And he was pretty sure witch hazel—generously applied by hand—would go a long way in soothing the burn.

If she wanted to stay with him for a while, he'd take good care of her. He wondered how she would take to his caretaking. He could be as good at it as she was. When he'd seen the horse go down with her, his heart had rocketed into his throat.

But then she'd stuck the horse like a pro, and Trace's heart had come down singing.

"How's my pole holdin' up?" he asked her.

"Solid," she said. "You're an excellent nailer."

"Jack-of-all-trades, master of none."

"Is bronc riding a trade?" She lowered herself off the rail and sat down on the patch of grass beside him. "Because if it is…"

"I'd call cowboying a trade and rodeo a profession. Cowboys have to be skilled at damn near everything that comes up on a ranch. I can buck out a bronc, easy, but I'm still workin' on being a real cowboy."

"Interesting." She was quiet for a moment. He stole a peek from beneath his hat and saw her giving Jack some love, rubbing his velvety nose. "What happens to a ranch that doesn't have its own cowboy?"

"It gets tagged a *farm*."

She laughed.

"You have a hired man," Trace recalled.

"He's a retired teacher."

"Well, hell, you've got a professional and a tradesman rolled into one."

"Grady grew up on a farm. He lives with his wife in Gillette. She keeps saying if the winters here get any worse she's moving to Arizona. I don't know what we'll do without him."

"*We?* Isn't that Mike's problem?"

"I write the checks," she reminded him.

"And Mike swipes the credit card."

She bristled. "He doesn't have to *swipe*. He has his own."

"Swipes on the machine," he clarified. "I would never suggest that Mike would take advantage. He has his own account?"

"Well…" She sighed. "I write all the checks."

He braced up on his elbow, pushed his hat back and looked her in the eye. "Why do you want another kid? You've got one big one, probably eats enough to feed two or three small ones."

She glared at him. And then she glanced away. Finally she burst out laughing. "You're all alike," she said merrily. "Not cowboys. *Men*."

"Oh, no, honey, that's just wrong." She was still chuckling, but he'd just thought up a way to sober her up. "Come live with me. I'll show you what you've been missing."

She thought he was kidding. He could tell by the way she was looking at him.

"You know what?" he continued. "You come into this world alone, and you go out alone, but you don't have to go it alone in between."

She tipped her head to one side as she went from point A to point B—amused to bemused.

"You're right—I'm not totally alone. I've got my brother, my father, a bunch of guys I can go down the road with whenever I need to save on gas. I've had some girlfriends." He swung his legs down and sat up, facing her. "But I've never found myself wanting to be with anyone day in, day out before. I want to be with you. I want to take you with me."

"Where?" She frowned and spoke guardedly. "For how long?"

"I don't know. As long as I can make you happy, I guess. Or until I break my fool neck. Like they say, I ain't asking you to back a horse that's only good for glue. But be with me now. Go down the road with me. Come back home with me."

"Trace, we hardly know—"

"We know we're good together, and we're learning each other. I want to keep it going." He lifted one shoulder. "It just feels right."

"I have...responsibilities."

"When are you going to stop letting them crowd out your dreams?"

"Most people have both. At this point in my life I have to be honest with myself about realities and possibilities."

"That's what I'm talkin' about. Sounds like a good plan." He backed off with a nod. "You oughta get to work on it."

She glanced at the fence. He had no clue what she was thinking, but he knew one thing. If she was going to let him down, she'd to it gently. She was that kind of woman. The kind he wanted to be with.

"Are we finished?" she asked quietly.

"We're finished here, but we still have a few promises to keep elsewhere." He offered her a hand up. "Cayenne for one. Cheyenne for two." He smiled, mostly to himself. "When the time comes for traveling music, I'm gonna write us a little ditty about Jack and Cayenne."

Chapter Nine

"We're going to Sinte," he told her the next morning.

Skyler turned away from the stove to get the rest of the announcement head-on. She'd gotten up in time to watch the sunrise and cook breakfast in the hope that the door to Trace's room was closed because he was getting needed sleep and he'd wake up and smell the coffee and come out of his corner smiling. It could happen, even though they'd slept in separate beds last night. An unspoken agreement, but she was chalking it up to her choice, which meant she had to do something to make up for it. In her experience, these things generally worked that way.

Oddly enough, he wasn't going for coffee first

thing. A kiss on her neck came first, just under her earlobe. It tickled.

"It's a town over on the other side of the Black Hills. My hometown." He helped himself to a strip of bacon, fresh from the skillet. "Ouch! Mmm. It's real close to the Double D, where you got Cayenne. We can stop there, too, if you want to."

"I'd like that, but I think we should call first."

"Call who?"

"We can't just drop in on people."

"Why not?" He took another piece of bacon and moved away. "Did you get coffee?"

"Not yet." She ran the spatula across the bottom of the skillet, through the scrambled eggs. "Because they won't be expecting us."

"I just got off the phone with Logan."

"Is something wrong?"

He laid one hand on her nape and set a cup of black coffee within her reach. "My father wants to meet you."

"Why? What did you tell him?" She watched him brace his butt against the edge of the counter adjacent to the stove. He was giving her that dancing-eyes bit as he sipped his coffee. *"What?"*

"I told him you used to be a princess, but you weren't the kind to let it go to your head too much." He shrugged. "Told him you were trying to get us pregnant." She scowled. *Truth or consequences?* "Isn't that the way it is nowadays? Not *she's* pregnant, but *we're* pregnant?" He chuckled. "Yeah, I'm kidding."

"It's not funny. You didn't say any of that, did you?"

"I told him I met a woman, and he said, 'Bring her home. And the horse she rode in on.'"

She scraped up the eggs again. Too much heat, too little focus. "He's probably more interested in the horse."

"He's seen the horse. He remembers it. We agree, you made the right choice."

"I do know something about horses." She started loading up two plates.

"I thought you wanted to meet him," he said as he took breakfast in hand.

"I do. And I want to show Sally some of the pictures we've taken." She took up her plate and headed for the table. "I thought we were going to work with Cayenne today."

"We will." He was shoveling his eggs down and hadn't moved from the space beside the stove. "Work off some energy before we load him."

"Would you come sit down, please?" she said quietly.

"Oh, yeah." He picked up his coffee and ambled over to the table. "Habit, I guess. Kinda nice, eating off a plate."

"And this is a great table." She'd claimed the end of the bench and left the chair for him.

"Came with the house. You sit down by yourself

and look way down to the end, you know how that guy on TV felt when his wife left and took the eight kids."

"*Jon* left," she said. "It's Kate who got the eight kids, the house and the show, and I can't believe you watch that."

"You stay in a hotel once in a while, you get a peek at cable TV. All I know is, these two get on TV because they have eight little kids, and then they split up." He lifted one shoulder. "That, and there was that long table."

"That's it in a television nutshell. Life unscripted." She smiled. "On with our own reality. The road awaits."

"Look, you wanna nitpick, could you pull in the claws?" He laid his fork down. "I'm not draggin' you anywhere." He reached under the table, found her hand and drew it into the open as he slid his chair back. He examined her manicured nails. "Damn. If you ever have a kid, you're gonna have to cut these."

"They're not that long."

"They're sharp." He released her hand, took up his dishes and gave her an odd look. "I'll call him back and tell him it's not a good time."

She closed her eyes and sighed. "I'm sorry. I don't know what's wrong with me."

"Hey," he said softly, touching her shoulder. "He just wants to meet you. He doesn't do interviews."

"I hope not."

"Yeah, we're not TV people." He smiled. "He's an author, and I'm a top hand in the PRCA, but we're like regular folks."

They cleaned up the kitchen together quietly. *We're good together.* What exactly did that mean? They worked well together. Everything they'd done together seemed to turn out well. He picked up where she left off and vice versa. Maybe they should do things together without talking, Skyler thought. Telling a man what you really wanted could be dicey. He might say, "Fine, honey," and let it ride. He might ignore you. Or he might treat you like a child and claim you didn't know what was good for you. Trace's attitude didn't seem to fall into any of those categories. He wasn't on board, but she wasn't feeling rejected, either.

How did he do that?

"I'll call and let Mike know where I'll be," Skyler said as she headed down the hall to pack her little bag.

"You do that."

Meaning what? She wanted to march back down the hall and point out to him that checking in was a good thing, and that anyone she lived with could depend on her to do just that. If she disappeared, she wanted to tell him, call out the bloodhounds. She probably *was* dead.

But she kept those thoughts to herself. If she had to tell him, he hadn't come far enough. Really and truly, they hardly knew each other. Being good together and learning each other sounded like something her father might have said. And her mother might have gone along with it because Dad was good with everybody, and he would gladly have spent his whole life learning people. It was a lovely idea—Dad had lots of lovely ideas—but it had nothing to do with responsibilities. He'd taken on the little things—patched up small holes, grew beautiful tomatoes, made fabulous vegetable soup—but he'd hated milking cows, which was a fatal flaw for a dairy farmer. He'd gone under. Drowned in milk and whiskey.

Trace was young, she told herself. He had plenty of time to get himself all set up while he was figuring people out, finding the right one for his one and only and making the pieces fit. She, on the other hand, had responsibilities. She wasn't set up, but she had a few things figured out, and one of them was that on any given day, body parts were easy to put together. But bodies were not the same from one day to the next. They aged or they became ill or the fit changed. And that little fact could be a big dream killer. She'd taken all the right steps and made careful choices, but *right* and *careful* had betrayed her.

Being dependable was all she knew. She had dependability to spare. Her sense of responsibility would easily cover for two people—mother and father—and that was where she'd decided to put her eggs—into the parenthood basket. She wasn't interested in following a man around the way her mother had done before she'd talked Dad into going back home and taking over his father's farm. It was a mistake to try to make a man over. And she was no longer interested in being beautiful and dutiful. She wanted to love and be loved for herself. Her below the skin and down to the core plain ol' reliable self.

But couldn't she afford to enjoy the good fit she'd found with Trace for a little while longer? Maybe the fit only went bad when you started trying to force it. Fresh start, he'd said, and while she wasn't sure such a thing was possible for the long haul, it seemed doable right now. She was trying to turn a corner in her life, and maybe she'd turned too fast, too sharp, too hard, but he was still willing to take a ride with her at the wheel. He was, without a doubt, a good man, and she wanted to meet the man who'd raised him.

She also wanted to meet the man who'd taught Trace everything he knew about horses, considering how much he knew. She was taking a break that nobody had to give her, and nobody was going to put any limits on it. She wasn't looking for a small break. She was looking for something worth taking a risk for, and risking big.

The drive to Sinte was over three hours' worth of scenic beauty and heavy silence. Trace wasn't surprised by the silence. He'd known all along that he was dealing with a complicated woman. What he hoped to gain with the trip was time. They'd had some good times. They needed some real time. And there was no more telling reality than the first time a guy took a woman home to meet the family. Especially when the family was Logan Wolf Track.

They stopped on the way to check in with Sally Drexler Night Horse, for whom Mustang Sally's Wild Horse Makeover Challenge was named. The side door opened on the barn and out came Sally—the small but never meek—leaning heavily on her cane. She waved when she saw them. Multiple sclerosis never appeared to dampen Sally's enthusiasm.

"What to my wondering eyes appears." Sally gave her visitors a bright-eyed once-over that was the adult version of *Skyler and Trace, sittin' in a tree...* Then she acknowledged Trace's flamingo stance. "I heard about your injury, cowboy. How're you doing? You gonna make it to Cheyenne?"

"As long as I can swing a leg over a bronc, I'm good for another go-round."

"Is he?" she asked Skyler.

"If he says so."

Sally glanced back and forth between the two of them and winked. "I tell you what, this contest was the best idea I ever had."

"You're bringin' out the best," Trace said. "Is Hank around?"

"No, but Logan was here this morning. He said you were bringing a new girlfriend home for his approval. I asked him if that was a Lakota rule, and he said the Lakota don't have rules. They have *ways*. So I never really got an answer." Sally adjusted her sunglasses. "Except he did say you hadn't brought a girl around to meet him since you were in high school."

"You're not helping, Sally." Trace glanced at Skyler. Big, dark glasses, tight lips. *Go easy, Wolf Track. Bring her on home.* "I keep telling her, she's not meeting the chief of the Great Sioux Nation." He smiled. "He should be, but there isn't one."

Sally rubbernecked for a look at the horse trailer. "You're not bringing that horse back, are you?"

"Oh, no. We're out to win this thing." Skyler looked at Trace and he gave her an *attagirl* wink. "I have a proposition for you, Sally."

"You can't keep the horse." Sally waved off the idea prematurely. "We're selling them after the contest is over. This is a fundraiser." She turned to Trace. "Logan already took his wife's mustang out of the running. He adopted it for her, lovesick bridegroom that he is. But I can't let any more go." Back to Skyler. "Logan helped us get more lease land from the tribe. And Mary's my best friend." Sally shrugged. "So sue me."

"Who would dare?" Trace said. "No, Skyler wants to help you out, too. And she's a hell of a photographer."

"Photographer?"

"I've taken some still shots and quite a bit of video," Skyler said.

"She's a real pro."

"Well, not…" Skyler touched Trace's shirtsleeve.

Thank you. "But I'm getting there. If you have time, I'd like to show you some of it."

"Time for pictures of my babies? You damn betcha."

"Because I have this idea." With encouragement from all sides, Skyler stepped closer. "About making a sort of a documentary video. Has anyone else approached you?"

"You're the first."

"Well, I'm sure I won't be the last, and I'm sure you'll be hearing from some *real* pros, but I just thought I'd—" Skyler punctuated her determination with a fist to the palm "—just *do* it. I'm just doing it." She shrugged. "And we'll see."

"How can I help?" Sally wanted to know.

"I'm focusing on Cayenne, and so far I have a video diary."

"Cayenne? Like the spice?" Sally grinned. "I like that."

"I'd like to set up some interviews, starting with you. Whenever you have time."

"Time to talk? I can always find time to talk." Sally nodded toward the corrals. "Turn Cayenne out in that empty pen over there, and let's have a look at your pictures. What do you want me to talk about? Have you ever seen that movie *Free Willy?* I love that movie." Skyler and Trace went about the business of unloading a wary mustang while Sally went right on brainstorming. "We can't call it *Free Cayenne* because we're gonna auction him off. But we could still have a scene where we turn some horses loose, and they take off, tails flying, and we all cheer. *Yay! Run free!*" She waved her hat. "It's okay if you show me in the wheelchair. Being all inspirational, of course. I always say, if you've got it, flaunt it." She grinned. "Schmaltz sells."

Sally's enthusiasm was a confidence builder. Skyler saw her pictures with new eyes. Video from the day she'd picked out her horse, from the work she'd done on her own and more recent video with Trace's voice behind the camera—all of it showed promise. *We could show this. We could add more of that.* The ideas poured in from all three sides, and nobody was more excited about them than Skyler was.

Trace begged off the offer of a meal. Logan was expecting them. It was Trace's turn to stare out the pickup's side window quietly as the fence posts and ditch grass flew past. They passed a sign that said Welcome to the Lakota Nation and another at the top of a hill marking five more miles to the town of Sinte.

From a distance it looked like most prairie communities—a collection of boxes all but lost in a sea of grass. As they drew closer, Skyler started framing shots mentally. Embraced by stalwart hills and overarching sky, there were community buildings of some substance, but the clusters of homes tended toward the ramshackle. Splendor and shabbiness in the same frame. Life.

Logan Wolf Track lived in a log house facing the highway. There was a round pen out back, much like the one Trace had built, but Logan's pole barn was made of metal and his paddock was smaller. A beautiful claybank mustang pricked his ears and monitored their approach from his vantage in the adjacent pasture.

Tall, lanky and darkly handsome, Logan met them at the door, ushered them in and shook hands with Trace first and then with Skyler as she was introduced simply by her first name.

Skyler launched what she considered to be protocol.

"I understand congratulations are in order. You just got married?"

"Thanks. I did. I'm a lucky man."

"Surprised the hell out of me." Trace nodded toward the kitchen table, and Skyler took a seat. "I didn't even get an invitation," he called out to his father, who was pouring coffee on the other side of the island divider.

"You got a call." Logan set cups on the table in front of each of his guests. "Kind of a shotgun affair. My wife's in the army."

"Who was holding the shotgun?" Skyler asked.

"The army," Logan said with a laugh. "Mary was home on leave and she had to get back to her post. But she's getting out soon. She's…" He took a seat at the table, folded his hands, fingers laced, and announced almost reverently, "We're having a baby."

"The hell," said Trace.

"Congratulations again," Skyler said, glancing at Trace. *Poor man. He thought his father's place would give him respite from any kind of baby talk.*

He shook his head in amazement. "Damn, you work fast."

"So Trace's gonna have a baby brother or sister in a few months." Logan was beaming. "What do you think of that?" he asked his son.

"I think it's fine." Trace sipped his coffee. He took another moment and then lifted one shoulder. "Hell, I think it's great. Have you told Ethan?"

"Haven't told anyone yet. Mary told her mother. You're my first." He grinned. "And it feels chest-swellin' good."

"So she's getting out of the army. Retiring?"

"She's not old enough to retire." Logan turned to Skyler. "My wife's a few years younger than I am. And I'm not old enough to retire." He chuckled. "Never will be. But Mary's been in the army more than ten years, and she's done more than her share in the Middle East, so she's taking a discharge. She's a dog handler."

"And Logan's on the Tribal Council." Trace glanced out the window. "I see you've got your mustang out back."

"You brought yours?"

"I always do what you tell me. You know that."

"How's the foot? You gonna be ready for Cheyenne?"

"Oh, yeah. You coming?"

"Wouldn't miss it."

"So what do you say we double-team Skyler?" Trace proposed. "She started the horse, and she's been doing the groundwork herself."

"I do what you tell me to do," she said. She wasn't sure she'd appreciate instructions from two Wolf Tracks at the same time.

"Ohan." Logan's tone said *aha.* "How's that workin' for you?" He caught her glancing at Trace. "Not for *him.* For you."

"I think it's going very well," she said. "But he gives you full credit. Oh, and I have a copy of your book, which backs him up on that. Will you sign it for me?"

"I like this woman." Logan's smile made Skyler feel chosen. "You don't be waiting on him if he's acting *unsica* over a little sprain."

"That's *pitiful,*" Trace explained, "which I'm not."

"No, you're not." Logan tapped the table with a flat hand. "Let's see what your mustang can do. What're you calling him?"

"Cayenne." The look on Trace's face read, *Don't blame me.*

"Cayenne? What's that, some newly recognized Indian tribe?"

"Close," Trace said. "It's red pepper. Sneaks up on you and burns like the devil."

Logan laughed. "I'll bet it's good for the heart."

* * *

They turned the mustang out into the round pen, and Skyler went through her beginning ground routine. Then she returned to the side of the ring, where Trace was holding the next piece of equipment—the longe line.

"Lookin' good," Logan told her.

"You think he'll take her on his back?" Trace asked.

"Damnedest thing," Logan said. "I can't get on our mustang yet, but Mary rode him already. Horses and women have a natural connection."

Trace looked at Skyler. She didn't say the words, but *What did I tell you?* was written all over her face.

"Yeah, let's put her up there today."

Skyler beamed.

Trace rode the fence beside his father while Skyler longed the horse. Logan had been his sounding board ever since he'd brought the family home. He seldom offered unsolicited advice, but unlike his brother, Trace wasn't shy about soliciting.

"Have you heard anything from my mother?"

Logan's brow furrowed. "Not since the divorce was final and I got the papers she signed." He didn't take his eyes off Skyler and Cayenne. "Why? Have you heard from her?"

"Not since she called and said she'd be coming to get us, but not for a while." He gave the idea a tongue clucking. "I didn't say anything. If she came, I wasn't going."

"You'd like to know what happened to her."

"Not really." It was a lie. He knew it, and he knew Logan knew it. "But I thought if anybody did…"

"I'd tell you if I did."

Trace watched the mustang canter at the end of Skyler's line. Life on the line. Two beautiful creatures. Maybe a third. It could happen. He was beginning to like the idea.

"You think she's dead?" he asked quietly.

"I don't think about her much anymore."

"But you married her," Trace said. "I never understood that."

"It seemed like a good idea at the time, and it brought me you two boys."

"You wanted kids?"

"I wanted your mother," Logan said. "She happened to have two kids. Some people say things happen for a reason. I say, things happen, and you take hold of the line and don't let yourself get run over. Down the road, maybe you can say things happen for a reason." He adjusted his hat—the cowboy's way of adjusting his thinking. "I wanted to do what was right, and it turned out pretty damn good."

"You were the best thing that could've happened to Ethan and me. I don't know if I've ever told you that, but it's true."

Logan nodded. It was the kind of acknowledgment he wouldn't take lightly. For Logan, words were pretty lightweight in the scheme of things.

"You wanna hear something crazy?" He gave a chin jerk toward the horse in the pasture. "That horse—we call him Adobe—he knew Mary was pregnant before she did."

Trace chuckled. "Did he slip you a note? Scratch out the word in the dirt?"

"Smart-ass. You're good, but you haven't come quite far enough. You understand their nature, but you don't respect the mystery. *Sunka wakan.* Spirit dog." Logan nodded. "That horse came to her, stood right up next to her—that wild horse—and he lowered his head right next to her belly." He looked at Trace. "Have you ever seen anything like that? It wasn't long after that we found out."

"When did she ride him?"

"Before she found out. His first time, too. Had nothing on his back before that. He took care of her like she was family." Logan lifted one shoulder. "'Course, if we'd known…"

"Trace, could you help me?" Skyler called. "I'm ready. Cayenne's ready. Boost me up?"

Trace hadn't noticed that Skyler had stopped working the longe line. She had the rope coiled, and she was rubbing Cayenne's neck. Trace quickly lowered himself down the fence and dropped into the pen on his good foot. Logan was right. Trace had the utmost respect for his father, but he didn't trust mysteries.

There was no way Skyler was getting on that horse.

Chapter Ten

In the days that followed, Trace stuck to his guns. Skyler was in charge of the groundwork, but nobody was going to ride Cayenne except him. He didn't want the horse to acquire any bad habits from the get-go. Skyler stopped objecting when she realized what his problem was. Whenever she thought about telling him she wasn't pregnant just to take him off the hook, the lie wouldn't come. She understood that she wasn't alone in the possibility-of-parenthood basket. Her eggs would just sit there without his input. And Trace wasn't about to deny his input.

When it came time to pack up for Cheyenne, her body gave her its answer. *Not this time*. She gave him the news in three simple words, uttered as tonelessly as she could manage. He said nothing. He put his hand behind her head, drew her to him and kissed her forehead. She tried to discern his thoughts from the look in his eyes, but she couldn't be sure whether it was *Thank you, Jesus* or *You have my sympathy, Skyler.* What she knew for certain was that this man would be a good father someday.

He asked her to share a room with him in Cheyenne. He had a camper that he could load onto the back of his pickup, but he also had a hotel reservation. One room. Everything else was booked. They could take the camper and she could have the room, or...

She told him to leave the camper at home.

He still favored his injured ankle when he wasn't thinking about it, or when he'd been on his feet a while. Skyler welcomed the opportunity to drive the pickup. He didn't need to put any stress on that ankle. And she needed to be needed just now, and not by the boy she'd raised, but by the man she...

...*loved.* There, she'd formed the word. Not aloud, but in her mind. It felt true.

He emerged from the hotel bathroom wearing brand-new blue jeans and a bright pink shirt. *Pink.* All she could say was, "Wow."

"You like it?"

"I'd wear it myself."

He grinned. "It goes with my lucky rabbit's foot. I need all the luck I can get today."

"Well, take it off and let me iron it," she said. "You bought it off the shelf."

"I know how to iron." He reached for his hat.

"I know you do, but it would be my pleasure to iron your shirt for you."

He put the hat back, set up the ironing board for her and caught her gaze while he unsnapped his pink shirt. He could read her mind. She didn't know which part he was reading, but the look in his eyes told her he was picking up serious vibes.

When they reached the arena, she saw another pink shirt. She snapped a picture. Behind the chutes there were more pink shirts.

"Did you boys call each other about this? *Hey, guys, what color should we wear today?*" Skyler laughed. "Or did the Cat in the Hat visit the locker room?"

"We don't have a locker room." Trace pointed to the sign on the crow's nest. Tough Enough to Wear Pink, it said, and the loop of a breast-cancer-awareness ribbon explained it all. "It's been going on for a few years. Big fundraiser for the PRCA." He smiled. "In some ways, I guess cowboys *are* all alike."

Skyler snapped a picture of the banner and a few more of cowboys doing their stretching routines and getting their equipment in order. She took pictures of the human ribbon the survivors and their families formed in the arena, and all the while she thought about Trace and his father and what kind of men they were. They were tough enough to be gentle. Tough enough to give all they had without worrying about what it might cost them. Tough enough to do the right thing.

For Trace, the right thing meant holding off on commitments he wasn't ready to make. Being with Skyler was one thing. Fatherhood was something else.

Which meant that Skyler had to get tough, as well.

Trace had the second-highest score in the first go-round, but he won the second, and he took first in bareback. It was a huge win. With a few more rodeos like this one he was a shoo-in for the National Finals and a good bet to take the championship. He had to keep "going down the road."

And he wanted her to go with him.

"I can't do this, Trace," Skyler told him on the drive back to Gillette, to her house, her responsibilities, her life. "I'm not a rodeo groupie or—what do you call those girls—a buckle bunny."

"I never took you for one. I wouldn't have been interested." He glanced over at the passenger's seat. "What can't you do? Go with me? Be with me?"

"I have to go home."

"To what?"

"What I know. Where I'm safe. Your road is a high place, and I need to be safe on the ground. I need to be necessary."

"You're becoming necessary," he said. "I'm not gonna say I can't live without you, but I will say I don't want to."

"And I'm not saying we can't be together. I want to see you as much as I can. As often as I can."

"Every day," he insisted. "Every day works for me."

"But not for me. I have to go home and help Mike figure out what to do with his cattle operation." She sighed. "Okay, it's for him to figure out. But I have to help get things in order. I have to—"

"You do what you have to do, then."

Little was said after that. He pulled into the yard at the ZQ, parked, shut off the motor, draped his wrists over the top of the steering wheel and sighed. "I guess this is where you get off."

"Is that it?"

"No. I'll call you."

"Okay."

"I'll stop back when you're ready to take Cayenne out under saddle."

"Okay."

He turned to her, hooked his arm around her neck and drew her to him for a fierce and hungry kiss. "I'm not letting you go," he said.

"Okay. I…." She wouldn't say it. He hadn't said it, and she refused to say it. "I can call you, too, can't I?"

"You damn well better."

There had been no calls in the weeks that passed between Cheyenne and the approaching deadline for the wild-horse-training competition. Skyler was riding Cayenne every day, and she was proud of the progress she'd made with him. He probably wouldn't win any prizes, but he was saleable, and she had done much of the work herself.

She could do more of it. More horses, more training for a purpose other than her own. She could help get them ready for someone else. She could help Trace build toward the time when he would turn his corner. When he called, she would offer. Three *ifs* about that call. It would come.

And when it did, she would have much to tell him. She was Mike's mother, but she was no longer his nanny. She'd decided to think of herself as his employee. She had given him notice, but it wasn't the two weeks' kind. It was more like a presidential advisor letting the big guy know that she was getting close to burnout on this job. She would lay out his options the way she saw them, but he would have to sit down with her and pay serious attention. Otherwise, she'd have the two weeks' notice on his desk by the following day.

There was real work to be done before the ZQ calf sale. Mike had decided to sell half the cows. He'd recognized that it was the only way to pay the bills. With only half the breeding stock left, the future of the ranch was in jeopardy, and she was pretty sure he recognized that, too. She thought it was salvageable, but saving it would take hard work and determination. It was time for her son to decide what he really wanted to do. She told him about her father. It was a story she'd kept to herself for a long time, protecting it from harsh lights and harsher judgments. Mike seemed to understand what telling the story meant to her, and he thanked her for it.

Skyler's video was another story. It was going to be a masterpiece. Or close to it.

It would stand up in any light, withstand all judgment because the subject was as big as the West, a vital part of its heritage, and she had a knack for finding and framing the right images. She had the patience to wait for them and the eye that could pick them out from the piles and piles of pixels she'd recorded. She wasn't sure how she was going to get it out there, but between her and Sally Night Horse, *the way forward* would be more than just a catchphrase.

She was listening to an interview she'd done with the wild-horse manager in Worland, where the Bureau of Land Management regional office was located, when she looked up through the office window and saw a familiar pickup headed for the house.

She was a mess. Hair stuck up in a ponytail, ratty T-shirt, bare feet. But she ran to the door, tore it open and struggled to collect herself at the sight of her cowboy standing there on her porch. No smile. No salutation.

"I'm here to help out," he told her. It sounded like an open-ended offer, and the look in his eyes said he was ready to fend off any objections, reject any exceptions.

She had none. All she really wanted to do was feast her eyes, but instinctively she launched into a report.

"Cayenne is taking a bit, changing leads quite nicely, learning to—"

He caught her in his arms and shut her up with a kiss, hard and fast at first—much like a rodeo event—but when she gave as good as she got, he slowed down and kissed gently, greeting her tongue with his, dropping back and then kissing again. And again.

"Not with the horse, unless that's what you need," he said finally. "I'll be your handyman. Your jack-of-all-trades. I don't know what you're gonna do with this place, but, hell, I'll help you cut your kid's steak for him if that's what it's gonna take. I want to help with whatever you need. So you can be with me."

"Be where?"

"Anywhere. I don't care. Like I said, it's not that I can't live without. It's just that I'd rather not."

"Me, too." She put her arms around him and hugged him hard. "I don't care either. I'll ride the rails with you if that's what you want."

"It isn't." In his eyes relief displaced the readiness to play defense, and he took her face in his hands. "I'm in love with you, Skyler. That's why I'm here. I want to marry you and train horses and play games and make babies and pictures." He laughed, probably because she was laughing, which was one of the many things that made them good together. "And baby pictures."

"I don't want to wait," she said. "And not because I can't wait. I can if I have to, but I don't want to. I want to get on with loving you, and I want our babies to come from loving each other. But—" she drew the breath she needed, the one that gave her pause to consider him "—we can work that out. I mean…I'm not the one wearing the condom."

He laughed so hard she was afraid he was going to fall down on the porch, so she pulled him inside, closed the door, pressed her forehead against his chest and gave him a playful punch in his quivering gut. "But I want the pants," she said.

"After I get yours."

"Would you believe me if I told you I had an allergy to latex?"

"Nope." He put his arms around her. "You think I *like* wearing the damn thing?"

"I think…" She looked up at him. "I think you're a good man. After we get the fall work done, I want you to take me away from here," she said. "Where can we go?"

"To the National Finals for starters," he told her. "And then we'll make a home together."

"Where?"

"Together. This is your house, right?" She nodded. "Is it the home you want?" She shook her head. "So we'll work that out, too, and we'll be together as much as we can while we're workin' it—" he charmed her with a sweet smile, teased her with a cocky wink "—baby. What do you say?"

"I'm ready, cowboy." She held him close again and whispered, "I'm so ready."

* * * * *

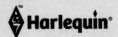
Harlequin®

SPECIAL EDITION

REQUEST YOUR FREE BOOKS!

2 FREE NOVELS PLUS 2 FREE GIFTS!

✦ Harlequin

SPECIAL EDITION

Life, Love & Family

HSE11

Harlequin® Blaze™ brings you
New York Times *and* USA TODAY *bestselling author*
Vicki Lewis Thompson with three new steamy titles
from the bestselling miniseries SONS OF CHANCE

Chance isn't just the last name of these rugged
Wyoming cowboys—it's their motto, too!

Read on for a sneak peek at the first title,
SHOULD'VE BEEN A COWBOY

Available June 2011 only from Harlequin® Blaze™.

"THANKS FOR NOT TURNING ON THE LIGHTS," Tyler said. "I'm a mess."

"Not in my book." Even in low light, Alex had a good view of her yellow shirt plastered to her body. It was all he could do not to reach for her, mud and all. But the next move needed to be hers, not his.

She slicked her wet hair back and squeezed some water out of the ends as she glanced upward. "I like the sound of the rain on a tin roof."

"Me, too."

She met his gaze briefly and looked away. "Where's the sink?"

"At the far end, beyond the last stall."

Tyler's running shoes squished as she walked down the aisle between the rows of stalls. She glanced sideways at Alex. "So how much of a cowboy are you these days? Do you ride the range and stuff?"

"I ride." He liked being able to say that. "Why?"

"Just wondered. Last summer, you were still a city boy. You even told me you weren't the cowboy type, but you're…different now."

He wasn't sure if that was a good thing or a bad thing. Maybe she preferred city boys to cowboys. "How am I different?"

"Well, you dress differently, and your hair's a little longer. Your face seems a little more chiseled, but maybe that's because of your hair. Also, there's something else, something harder to define, an attitude…"

"Are you saying I have an attitude?"

"Not in a bad way. It's more like a quiet confidence."

He was flattered, but still he had to laugh. "I just admitted a while ago that I have all kinds of doubts about this event tomorrow. That doesn't seem like quiet confidence to me."

"This isn't about your job, it's about…your…" She took a deep breath. "It's about your sex appeal, okay? I have no business talking about it, because it will only make me want to do things I shouldn't do." She started toward the end of the barn. "Now, where's that sink? We need to get cleaned up and go back to the house. Dinner is probably ready, and I—"

He spun her around and pulled her into his arms, mud and all. "Let's do those things." Then he kissed her, knowing that she would kiss him back, knowing that this time he would take that kiss where he wanted it to go. And she would let him.

Follow Tyler and Alex's wild adventures in
SHOULD'VE BEEN A COWBOY
Available June 2011 only from Harlequin® Blaze™
wherever books are sold.